CAMP
AVERAGE

Away Games

For Karen, Karen, and Sarah

Text © 2021 Craig Battle

Owlkids Books acknowledges the financial support of the Canada Council for the Arts, the Ontario Arts Council, the Government of Canada through the Canada Book Fund (CBF) and the Government of Ontario through the Ontario Creates Book Initiative for our publishing activities.

Published in Canada by
Owlkids Books Inc.
1 Eglinton Avenue East
Toronto, ON M4P 3A1

Published in the United States by
Owlkids Books Inc.
1700 Fourth Street
Berkeley, CA 94710

Library of Congress Control Number: 2020941423

Library and Archives Canada Cataloguing in Publication
Title: Away games / Craig Battle.
Names: Battle, Craig, 1980- author.
Series: Battle, Craig, 1980- Camp Average (Series)
Description: Series statement: Camp average
Identifiers: Canadiana 20200285645 | ISBN 9781771474054 (hardcover)
Classification: LCC PS8603.A878 A95 2021 | DDC jC813/.6—dc23

Edited by Sarah Howden
Cover design by Alisa Baldwin
Cover illustration by Josh Holinaty

Manufactured in Altona, MB, Canada, in September 2020, by Friesens
Job #268678

A   B   C   D   E   F

Publisher of Chirp, Chickadee and OWL
www.owlkidsbooks.com

Owlkids Books is a division of bayard canada

CAMP AVERAGE

AVERAGE

AWAY GAMES

CRAIG BATTLE

Owlkids Books

TABLE OF CONTENTS

CHAPTER
1

"SAFETY FIRST!"

"What are you waiting for, Pat?" Miles Holley whispered to his friend. "The countdown finished a whole countdown ago. Push the button."

"Quiet!" Patrick Meyer said in an exaggerated hiss. He closed his eyes and tilted his head back, breathing deeply. "I'm savoring this."

The two boys were standing just beyond second base of the senior baseball field at Camp Avalon (Camp Average, to those in the know). Pat, the taller of the two, held an oblong black control box with a wire jutting out of one end. The wire snaked along the bright green grass until it reached a blue-and-red ESTES Expedition model rocket mounted on a makeshift launchpad in shallow center field.

Miles, Camp Average's foremost rocketry aficionado, mustered an embarrassed smile as he felt the eyes of his rocketry instructor and two other campers on him.

"'Savoring,' Pat? I think you mean 'spoiling,'" he said

under his breath, pushing his glasses back on his face and pinning them to the bridge of his nose.

"You would know!" Pat grunted. Then he turned his attention back to the control box. "Now, where is this button you mentioned?"

It was only the first day of camp, and Miles was already worn out by Pat's low-wattage pranks—not to mention regretful that he'd agreed to let Pat do the honors for his first launch of the summer.

"Give it to me," Miles whispered, the fake smile hurting his cheeks.

"No, no," Pat said, examining the underside of the control box. "I've almost got the hang of this."

That did it. Miles casually rubbed the back of his head to fake Pat out, then lunged at the control box with both hands, accidentally pressing the button in the process.

"Hey!" Pat shouted indignantly. "Safety first!"

Inside the rocket, the propellant ignited, generating enough exhaust gas to thrust the vessel skyward.

"Nice one!" Pat exclaimed as the rocket started its thousand-foot climb. "I should help you out with more of these things."

Just as Miles breathed a sigh of relief, he felt a little breeze ruffle his hair. "The forecast didn't say anything about wind," he mumbled to himself. "This means ..."

The moment the rocket's nose cone popped off and its parachute emerged, the wind picked up and pushed it away from the field toward the center of camp. Miles darted across the right-field line, between the outfield fence and the bleachers, tracking the rocket in the sky. The wind wasn't strong enough to drag it all the way out to the lake, but that didn't mean the rocket was safe.

"Wait up!" Pat shouted from behind him, dropping the controller in the grass.

"No time!" Miles shouted over his shoulder. "It's heading toward the ball-hockey court!"

A pain developed in his gut as he envisioned the worst for his rocket: landing on the court and getting run over by ten helmeted kids looking out for orange plastic balls, not cardboard rockets.

But there was no direct route from the senior baseball field to the ball-hockey court. Unless …

"Through the woods!" he shouted.

Miles cut behind the fence and along the line of trees that sat behind it. Then he plunged into them and down the hill, branches ricocheting off him as he went. His steely eyes never wavered as pine needles hit his glasses and got stuck in the frames.

"Ow!" Pat shouted from behind him. "*Ow!* COME ON!"

Miles hit level ground at a dead sprint and bolted

through an active ropes course, craning his neck and fruitlessly scanning the dense canopy of trees for any sign of his rocket.

"Look out!"

Miles saw a life pass before his eyes—just not his own life. Instead, it belonged to a kid on a zip line, who missed him by inches.

"Look—"

"Oof!"

Apparently, Pat wasn't so lucky with the next zip liner.

Miles heard the two kids land in a heap, but he didn't slow his own momentum. While Pat stumbled to his feet, Miles dropped to the ground and slid full speed under a climbing wall, then sprang up to continue running.

"There it is!" he shouted as he emerged back into open air and regained sight of the rocket.

But as the ball-hockey court came into view across a large green space, the boys heard a cheer rise up and saw what seemed like a hundred kids gathered around the boards.

"What's with all these people?" Pat asked.

A thought dawned on Miles. "Maybe it's the Hortonia kids?"

There were four big sports camps in the area. Camp Killington specialized in baseball. Roundrock dominated

4

in basketball. And Hortonia lived and breathed ball hockey. Camp Average didn't have a sports specialty, and it showed in how its teams rarely won at anything—hence the name. But this year, the kids who went there were still one up on Hortonia… who didn't have a camp.

"Still can't believe they're staying in our lodge," Pat grunted between breaths.

"The winter was so bad and lasted so long, they couldn't finish the renovations they started last fall," Miles panted. "Where do you expect them to go?"

"I don't know," Pat wheezed. "Somewhere else? Anywhere but here? There are so many options!"

As the pair approached the court, Miles alternated between fresh terror and relief.

At its current trajectory, the rocket was going to land on the court.

But at least there was only one person on it.

But that person was Garth Fortin.

Miles knew Garth from the junior-camp baseball tournament two summers earlier. He was the pitcher on the Hortonia team, and he had harassed Miles's friend Mack at a camp social before Pat had stepped in to break things up.

At the moment, Garth was lining up a slap shot in the far end of the court—the same end the rocket, now just twenty feet from the ground, had chosen for its landing.

"Wait!" Miles shouted, jumping over the boards at the opposite end.

But Garth was already winding up, seemingly unaware of the rocket about to set down between him and his target.

In his peripheral vision, Miles caught a glimpse of his friends at the side of the court. The stricken looks on their faces told him everything he needed to know.

The rocket was as good as gone.

Garth brought his plastic hockey stick down with electrifying speed.

WHACK!

Miles cringed as the orange ball hurtled through the air …

And missed his rocket by an inch.

The object of Miles's affection—the item he'd spent weeks building to exact specifications—simply twisted in the air as it fell the final two feet to earth, landing safely on the bluish-gray concrete court.

"Fifty-three miles per hour!" a deep-voiced adult shouted into a megaphone. "We have a winner!"

Miles barely registered this as he tore past a flexing, fist-pumping Garth. First inspecting, then lifting, then nuzzling the rocket with his cheek, he walked off the court toward his waiting friends, who didn't seem nearly as relieved as he was.

"Oh, Miles," said Nicole Yen, his friend from back home. She had started coming to Camp Average the summer before, when it had finally been opened up to girls. "I'm so sorry."

"What?" Miles asked, examining the object in his arms. "The rocket is fine. Not a scratch on it."

"Not the rocket," explained Makayla Monroe, Nicole's best friend. "The cabin."

"What about the cabin?" asked Pat, sidling up to the two girls. "Does ours need renovations, too? Do we have to go live in the Hortonia lodge?"

"Not exactly," said Willy "Wi-Fi" Reston, squeezing between Nicole and Makayla, an ability he had gained only the summer before, having finally overcome an all-but-crippling fear of physical contact with girls. "But the reality isn't much better."

Miles's analytical gaze bounced around his friends' anxious faces. "Will someone *please* tell me what's going on?"

Before he got an answer, Garth brushed by his shoulder and hopped over the boards.

"See you later, roomie!" he called as he walked away.

Roomie?! Miles thought sneeringly. *That'll be the—*

The small boy's eyeballs nearly popped out of his skull. "No!"

Setting her voice to "maximum soothe," Nicole reminded

Miles that there were two empty beds in his cabin. This fact he knew all too well. Those beds should have been occupied by two of his best friends, but he couldn't think about that right now for fear of tearing up.

"Evidently someone here thought it was cruel to make all the Hortonia kids sleep in the lodge when there were two beds just sitting there," said Nicole. "So camp administrators let the Hortonians decide which campers got them. They chose to settle it with a slap shot competition."

By now, Garth was a few hundred feet away. But his perfectly timed burp still rang out all the way back to them.

Miles groaned. "They couldn't have had a table manners contest?" he asked.

Nicole, Makayla, and Wi-Fi burst out laughing.

"Good one, Miles," Pat said, crossing his arms. "But just because I launched a rocket, that doesn't mean you get to be the funny one!"

The dinner bell blared across camp. Miles climbed over the boards and slumped toward his cabin like it was the principal's office.

"Don't worry," said Nicole, reading his face. "Garth won't have moved in ... yet."

Miles, Pat, and Wi-Fi split off from the rest of the group and made their way to cabin 23. Now that they were thirteen years old, they'd made it to senior camp. That meant their new living quarters contained nine single beds separated by an equal number of tall wooden dressers—eight for campers and one for their lone counselor. No more bunk beds. No more plastic bins. No more two-counselor setup.

Crossing the threshold, Miles noted with relief that Garth hadn't moved in yet. Instead, Nelson Ramos—*the* Nelson Ramos, the famous YouTuber and king of the unboxing video—was unpacking five polo shirts in different colors. And Spike and Mike, the Triplett twins, were playing soccey (basically ball hockey with a soccer ball) in the main aisle between the beds.

Sitting on his own bed by the front door, Laker, a counselor in his early twenties whose real name nobody at Camp Average had ever had any use for, held a pillow in his hands. "I swear," he said, "if a *fifth* soccer ball hits me in the face, so help me …"

As the boys entered the room, Mike stopped the ball under his foot.

"We heard …" he began.

"… cheering," finished his brother.

Nelson straightened. "What'd we miss?" Examining Miles's miserable expression, he furrowed his brow. "And I keep meaning to ask … where's Mack?"

CHAPTER
2

"ARE WE HAVING OYSTERS?"

Andre Jennings studied the silverware in front of him. There were three forks, two knives, one spoon, and one … something that looked like a mini two-pronged pitchfork.

He elbowed the kid sitting next to him in the Camp Killington clubhouse and pointed at the strange utensil.

"I think a bunch of tiny Aquamen lost their tridents," he joked.

The kid scoffed. "It's an oyster fork," he said. "Duh."

Andre made a face. "Are we having oysters?"

The kid shook his head and looked away, ignoring the question. Andre tugged at the collar of his black dinner jacket, which he'd found in a clear plastic sheath in the closet of his dorm room not ten minutes earlier.

It was dinnertime on his first day at Killington, and he was already feeling out of place.

Andre was seated at table number one, which was covered in the cleanest white tablecloth he'd ever seen and surrounded by the best baseball players in camp. Among them was Terry Dietrich—nephew of Major League Baseball Hall of Famer Jeffrey Dietrich, the camp's most famous alumnus. To his scouts and fans, Terry was better known by his uncle's nickname, Deets. But to Andre, Deets—the large boy with the bulging biceps and ego to match—was simply the reason he was here.

Andre had attended Camp Average since he was eight years old. But at the end of last summer, he'd been forced to call Deets for a favor—he and his teammates needed a short-notice ride to a basketball tournament, and Killington was the only camp in the area with its own bus. Deets had agreed to help, but only when Andre, a superstar baseball player himself, offered to switch to Killington in return.

Now here he was, a few miles from the place where he should have been spending his summer, trying to ignore the sinking feeling in his stomach as Deets bounced between conversation topics as varied as batting stances and batting gloves.

"And don't get me started on batting cages!" Deets exclaimed as his table neighbor nodded at him with fawning eyes.

Soon, waitstaff in all-black outfits poured out of the clubhouse kitchen, delivering individually catered plates from preset meal plans. Andre had to wait only a few moments before a waiter plopped a giant plate of lasagna down in front of him. He stabbed the lasagna with one of his three forks.

Then the kid next to him whacked him on the shoulder.

Andre dropped the fork and cast a confused look at the kid, who was staring intently across the table at Deets, still talking all things batting-related.

"What?" Andre whispered.

After a long minute, Deets turned away from his conversation partner and shoveled some rice and beans into his mouth. On cue, everyone else began eating as well, and suddenly the room was a symphony of glasses clinking and silverware hitting white china.

"And people say Camp Average is strange," Andre whispered to himself, finally taking a bite of his favorite food. Within minutes, every morsel was gone. A dessert course was similarly served and devoured.

When the meal was over, the adults stood from their tables and formed a long line at the front of the room.

"Hello, boys," said a smiling gray-haired man. He wore a Killington polo shirt tucked into khaki shorts, and his calf muscles seemed to be as big around as his head. "For those who don't know me, my name is Maxwell. I'm the director here at Camp Killington."

Maxwell introduced each of the adults at the front of the room, never faltering with a name or a bio. Finally, he turned back to the baseball players themselves. "I hope you all have a great summer and help us continue our winning ways," Maxwell said. "To give you newcomers a better idea of our legacy, I offer the following video." He smiled again. "Please get comfortable. There's a lot of ground to cover, and there'd be even more if only we hadn't lost the photos."

Andre sighed deeply as the players around him chuckled in appreciation. Then the lights dimmed, and the front wall became a giant movie screen. Dramatic classical music filled the room as a simple title card appeared: "1955 All-Camp Junior Baseball Tournament Champions." It was followed by sepia images of boys with big smiles and greased-up hair swinging thin wooden bats and making grabs with puffy brown ball gloves. When a photo of the same group of boys holding a trophy appeared, the campers in the room stood and cheered.

Next came a second title card: "1956 All-Camp Junior Baseball Tournament Champions." A familiar-looking batch of photos zoomed by on the front wall, and Andre's eyes began to glaze over.

The song ended, and the screen went blank.

"Phew," Andre said quietly.

Then another song started. On the screen: "1958 All-Camp Junior Baseball Tournament Champions." The slideshow moved on like that, skipping very few years—and none at all after 1985, when Jeffrey Dietrich appeared. The campers cheered hard for their most famous alumnus, but they found yet another volume level for the 2018 team, which boasted a ten-year-old Deets.

Then another title card: "2019 All-Camp Junior Baseball Tournament Runners-Up."

And … nothing. The music cut out and the screen went blank. Several seconds passed before another picture finally appeared on the wall.

Andre involuntarily sucked in a breath.

This picture was different.

This picture he recognized.

This picture was of him.

More accurately, it was of him and his Camp Average teammates, hoisting the familiar trophy. They were grinning their faces off in sleeveless orange T-shirts, arms around each other's shoulders—a team that no one had expected to win.

Andre smiled despite himself, then scanned the area around him and discovered he was the only one still looking at the photo.

The adults were looking at their feet.

And everyone else was looking at him.

It was no secret that Andre had played a big part in the Camp Average win. He'd pitched the whole game, hit a ninth-inning double, scored the go-ahead run, and thrown the bullet that beat Deets to home plate for the final out.

His cheeks burning, Andre pressed his chin to his chest and waited for the moment to end. But the moment refused.

Suddenly, though, the silence was broken by a sound that was as jarring as an ambulance siren. Someone was *clapping*.

Andre whirled in his seat, seeking the source of the noise.

The clapper was standing next to a table stuck so far in the back of the room it might as well have been in the kitchen. He was tall and thin, with green eyes and a mop of brown hair, wearing a light gray hoodie, flower-print shorts, and flip-flops—the only kid in the room without a black dinner jacket.

Andre recognized him as Mackenzie Jones.

His best friend.

"Yeah!" Mack shouted as his clapping picked up in intensity. "LET'S GET IT!"

Andre's brain crashed, a blank computer screen with a question mark in the center of it. Somehow … his best friend … was here … at *Killington* … making a fool of himself.

The assembled kids shook their heads in disgust. Andre slumped in his chair, not knowing whether he wanted to tackle Mack or hug him.

Or both.

Finally, the music kicked back in, ushering in a final slide: "2020 All-Camp Junior Baseball Tournament Champions."

Andre's new campmates stopped staring at Mack and jumped back up, their hands hammering together.

The final batch of photos passed by, and the slideshow came to an end.

Maxwell stood.

"And that's that," he said, seemingly having forgotten Mack's little interlude. "That's who we are. That's who *you* are." Then he turned and pointed out the window. "But it's getting late."

Andre hadn't noticed, but the sun had already gone down and curfew was only minutes away.

"Go get some sleep," Maxwell said. "Tomorrow, we train."

Andre rushed outside through the throngs of kids, craning his neck to find—

WHUMP!

He looked up and saw he'd run face-first into Mack, who stood there grinning at him.

"How are you real?!" Andre shouted as he rubbed his cheek. "There's no way you're real! You don't go to this camp."

Like Andre, Mack normally went to Camp Average. "Well, neither do you," he shot back playfully, a large black duffel bag at his feet. "Not usually."

"You know what I mean!" Andre shouted. "I made a deal and I have to be here. You don't."

Mack shrugged. "I couldn't talk you out of it," he said. "But I also couldn't let you do it alone."

Andre slumped down in the grass, an awed look on his face. By now, there were only a few stragglers around, exiting the clubhouse in the waning light of day.

"But … how did you get in?"

Mack rolled his eyes. "Thanks for the vote of confidence."

"You know what I mean! They take only a handful of new kids a year. They didn't make me try out because Deets vouched for me, but the process is supposed to take months."

Again Mack shrugged. "So I tried out for months."

"There are aptitude tests and psych evaluations!"

"One of the officials I met said I have a future in business."

"Taking grounders for days! Hitting off the tee for hours!"

"Turns out I have a decent power bat when I'm not trying to ditch practice to go waterskiing." Mack mimed hitting a home run. "They liked that coming from a prospect who plays second base."

Andre shook his head. "Only you could pull this off."

"And only at the last minute," Mack added. "They didn't tell me I'd been accepted until a few days ago, and I didn't get here until dinnertime. I haven't even been to my dorm yet." Mack pointed at his duffel. "If I'd known earlier, I might have told you."

"*Might* have?" Andre asked, cocking an eyebrow.

Mack grinned. "Probably not," he said. "The look on your face when you saw me in the clubhouse was too good to pass up."

Andre's face darkened. The memory of Mack drawing the ire of their new campmates was fresh in his mind. "About that ..." he said.

"What?" Mack asked incredulously. "They looked ready to attack! I had to take the heat off you."

Andre shook his head. "No," he said, "you didn't."

Mack furrowed his brow as Andre's mind flooded with the events of the past two summers, when they'd often chosen the path of most resistance. He was more than ready for a new strategy.

"I've been thinking a lot about this," Andre continued. "If I—*we*—just try to fit in here, they'll forget where we used to go to camp. Then maybe we can have a normal summer."

"You really believe that?" Mack asked.

Andre nodded solemnly. "I also believe that if we keep reminding them we're different, they'll keep treating us that way."

"Or they could learn to deal with it," Mack mumbled.

"Mack!" Andre said.

"Okay, okay," Mack said. He took a breath. "I get it. No more hero stuff. But I—"

"FRESH MEAT, DEAD AHEAD!"

Mack and Andre turned to see a white golf cart zooming toward them along the clubhouse pathway. Taking a half step back, Mack couldn't make out who was driving.

"Is that … ?" he mouthed before the cart screeched to a stop, its front bumper just a couple of feet away from Mack's shins.

"Deets," Andre sighed.

"Hey, *bestfriends*"—Terry Dietrich said the two words

like they were one—"get in. You're going to miss curfew." Then he leveled his eyes at Andre. "And you're leaving butt imprints on the lawn."

Andre stood. He looked behind him to find two cheek-sized imprints in the perfectly manicured grass.

"Going once ..." Deets said, looking at the time on his smartphone.

Andre and Mack shared a glance. There was only one empty seat. Mack shrugged, then flopped into the back of the cart with his duffel bag, his long legs dangling. Andre climbed in next to Deets.

"Like the golf cart?" Deets asked, jamming his foot onto the pedal and taking off down the concrete path. "I got the idea from your old camp director. What was his name? Wilson?"

"Winston," Mack and Andre said in unison.

"Right. *Winston.* Dude's a legend around here. The stuff he pulled on you guys ..."

Two summers before, Winston Smith had strolled into Camp Average in his red short shorts and high white socks, determined to turn the campers into mindless winning machines. He'd started by making competitive sports mandatory and eventually resorted to closing down all non-competitive activities.

"Is it true he released an ant colony into your archery

range to trick you into playing basketball for him?" Deets asked as they whizzed by one gazebo after another.

"Well, yes and no," Mack said warily. "He *said* there was an ant infestation, but he made that up—along with everything else."

Deets shook his head, a smile on his face. "Classic," he said.

Andre's cheeks burned. This wasn't his favorite subject. When Mack had decided to fight back against Winston by sabotaging the boys' and girls' basketball teams last summer, he had tried to protect Andre by leaving him out of the plan. That deception had nearly cost them their friendship.

"Where's Wilson now?" Deets asked.

"No one's heard from *Winston* since we finally proved what he was up to," Andre said.

From the back of the golf cart, Andre heard Mack whisper, "And hopefully no one ever does."

CHAPTER
3

"YOU GUYS ARE GOING TO GET ALONG"

Deets slammed on the brakes outside a building marked "Ruth," which resembled a place the real Babe Ruth might have lived in during his playing days. It was bright white and had four thick columns stretching from the ground to the top of the second floor.

"This is us," Deets said as they climbed out of the golf cart. Then he pointed a thick finger at Mack's chest. "Not *you*."

"No." Mack fished a piece of paper from the pocket of his hoodie. "I'm in … the Mendoza building," he read.

Andre snickered in spite of himself.

"What?" Mack asked.

"Mendoza," he said apologetically. "The Mendoza Line."

"What's the Mendoza Line?"

Andre shared an eye-rolling glance with Deets. "Mario Mendoza hit, like, .200 his entire big-league career.

Nowadays, if you're not hitting .200, you're said to be 'below the Mendoza Line' … and that's not good."

"So *I'm* in the dorm named after the avatar for mediocre hitting," Mack mused. "And *you're* in the dorm named after the greatest baseball player ever?" He thought for a second. "Seems about right."

Deets groaned, then disappeared through the door of the Ruth building.

"I think you're that way," Andre said, pointing down the row of dorms. "See you tomorrow?"

"You know it," Mack said.

The two boys high-fived and performed a kind of full-body shrug—their Camp Average handshake. Then, as Andre traced Deets's steps into their fancy new living quarters, Mack shouldered his duffel bag and continued down dorm row. Moving with a swarm of boys in black suit jackets, he passed by three identical two-story brick buildings: Mays, named for Hall of Fame outfielder Willie Mays; Koufax, after Dodgers great Sandy Koufax; and Dietrich, in honor of Deets's uncle, Jeffrey.

The crowd thinned out with each building, until Mack was among just a handful of others headed toward Mendoza. Finally, he spied the place he'd be spending his nights. It was set back from the path and looked like a downtown doctor's office with its brownish-gray walls, steel window frames, and frosted-glass door that had matted weeds growing in front of it.

Mack followed his fellow Mendoza residents through the door. Inside, he found a cavernous room with yellowing walls and cracked tile floors. In one of two rickety wicker chairs sat a twenty-something man staring intently at his smartphone. He had tan skin and spiky brown hair, and he was wearing a navy-blue staff T-shirt—evidently, he was Mendoza's dorm supervisor. He seemed oddly familiar, but Mack couldn't place him.

"My-name's-House-check-your-name-off-the-curfew-sheet," the man said flatly every few seconds, like a live version of the world's most boring GIF. "My-room's-at-the-end-of-the-hall-if-you-need-anything."

Mack checked off his name, took note of his room assignment, and proceeded down the hall until he found the right number. He took a breath, pushed open the door, and immediately slammed it against something just inside.

WHAM!

"Hey!" called an unseen boy from the other side of the door. "Slow it down, Flash."

Leaning into the doorway, Mack had a clear view of a cheap bunk bed on the far side of the room. On the top bunk was a kid with a shaved head, light brown skin, and a round belly. He sat cross-legged with his back against the wall, a large black baseball glove in his lap.

Clearly Mack's roommates had beaten him back.

"Uh," Mack said, embarrassed, "hi?"

The kid on the top bunk opened his mouth, but he didn't get the chance to say anything.

"Is that a question?" remarked a second boy from behind the door.

Mack squeezed into the room and closed the door behind him. His other roommate had dark hair and straight eyebrows. He was cradling a tablet on a single bed—the solid object that had stopped the door midway—and re-watching footage of a single baseball swing. The batter in the video appeared to be him.

"Hey, sorry about the door. I'm Mack."

"Good for you." The boy ran his index finger along the video's track bar, studying the swing in slow motion. "I'm Reo Mori. The chatterbox on the top bunk is Benny. I didn't get a last name."

"Nice to meet you guys," Mack said, looking from one to the other. Then his eyes settled on the wall. "Nice, uh, poster."

Above Reo's bed was a large framed picture of Deets—*their* Deets, not the baseball Hall of Famer.

"That's not mine," Reo said absently.

"But you did choose the bed underneath it."

Reo paused the video and looked up at the poster. "That's true."

Mack tried changing the subject a second time. "You guys made it here fast," he said. "I even got a ride partway."

"You think I'm just going to wander back and let people see me coming in here?" Reo snorted.

"What's wrong with here?" asked Benny, finally joining the conversation.

"Are you serious?" Reo asked.

"Yeah?" Benny replied warily.

"Another random question mark. You guys are going to get along." Reo put down the tablet. "Look, it's a tier system. The best senior players go in the Ruth building. They get the nicest rooms and the most opportunities to show the coaches what they can do."

This wasn't news to Mack, but it was to Benny, who suddenly looked like a kid who didn't have enough change to buy the toy he wanted. Still, Mack felt a surge of pride for Andre. Their campmates may have viewed him as an outsider, but the people who chose the room assignments respected his game.

"The next best go in Mays, and so on down the row," Reo continued. "The worst go here. You guys should take it as an insult."

Mack raised an eyebrow. "But you shouldn't?"

"No, I shouldn't," he said condescendingly. "I had the flu when tryouts were going on and got in on the word of my coach back home. Until I prove the administrators made the wrong call, I'm here … with *you*."

As Reo returned to his tablet, Mack couldn't help but see the room as he did—a kind of particleboard prison cell. He looked through the vertical blinds out the open window and saw only the brick facade of the Dietrich building.

At the sound of a truck roaring by on the road outside camp, Mack looked to Benny, but he found the boy had already lain down facing the wall.

This was something Mack hadn't prepared for. That spring, as he'd mentally steeled himself for the summer at Killington, he had always pictured himself bunking with Andre. Even if they were stuck with a bunch of guys who hated their guts, at least they'd have each other.

He hadn't spent even one second imagining bunking *only* with people who hated his guts.

Mack dragged his duffel bag across the room to the bunk below Benny's. There were no bins or drawers to unpack things into, and his roommates' bags were still full and sitting on the ground.

He pushed a black dinner jacket in a plastic sheath

and a bursting welcome backpack from his bunk onto the floor. Then he dug his sleeping bag out of his duffel, threw it on his bed, and lay on top of it.

One day down. Forty-one to go.

☙

Mack woke up with a start. He'd been having a nightmare about his campmates putting on black dinner jackets and vanishing into thin air, and he felt like he'd barely slept. But he could tell by the light pouring in through the vertical blinds that it was morning.

He took a breath and rolled onto his side, scanning his foreign surroundings to reacquaint himself. Everything was beige, from the blinds to the beds to the floor, where he found the sleeping bag he must have thrown off in the night.

He thought about his friends waking up a few miles down the road—the familiar faces, the jokes, and the pranks—and wished he could bring a little piece of that experience here.

He wiggled his toes and discovered he had fallen asleep in his socks. He yanked them off his feet and got a sudden sense of déjà vu.

Socks.

In his hand.

On the first day of camp.

Mack's eyes popped open. He looked to Reo, who was still asleep on his bed, half upright and slumped over, his tablet resting beside him.

Maybe he could bring a little Camp Average here after all.

Mack gently lowered his feet to the ground and crossed the room. He leaned over, placing first one sock and then the other on Reo's head. Reo didn't move.

Mack straightened and pivoted, a smile on his face as he crept back to his bed. Then he looked up and saw that Benny was awake, seeming both interested and confused.

As soon as Mack flopped onto his bed, he saw Benny's feet appear on the ladder from the top bunk. He, too, lowered himself quietly to the floor.

"It's on," Mack whispered.

Mack watched Benny tiptoe to Reo's bed, where he leaned over, picked both socks off the boy's head, and dropped them to the floor.

"Not funny," Benny mouthed as he crossed back to the bunk bed, a hurt look on his face, and climbed back up the ladder.

So much for tradition, Mack thought.

Not long after, Reo woke up with a snort and scanned

his surroundings. "Pick up your socks," he growled at his roommates. "I'm not your mother."

Ten minutes later, he and Benny both left for breakfast. As soon as Mack heard the door click closed, he threw his feet to the floor and grabbed the welcome backpack. He unzipped the bag and pushed past the water bottle and T-shirts inside until he found a narrow box in plastic wrapping.

"Bingo."

Mack tore into the package and removed a brand-new eight-inch tablet, which the camp website had said would be used for customized daily video instruction. But he had another use for it.

He logged into the camp network, typed an address into an app, and hit the video call button.

"Please pick up, please pick up, please pick up," Mack mumbled.

Just as he was about to give up, he heard a voice on the other end.

"Hello?"

"Pat!" Mack said. "Is that you?"

"Is this thing on?" said Pat, holding the tablet so close to his face that Mack could see only his hairline.

"Pat, this is serious!" Mack shouted. "I don't have much time!"

"This is your mother speaking. You are go for Mom."

Grading on the curve, this counted as a sophisticated joke for Pat, who lived for them. Normally, his comedic repertoire consisted of putting sleeping kids' hands in water and asking unsuspecting people to help him find a silver dollar he hadn't actually lost. Posing as Mack's mother was at least a new one.

Wi-Fi grabbed the tablet and repositioned it so the shot included him as well as Miles, Nelson, Spike, and Mike, who all crowded around.

"Hey, guys," Mack said, a wistful note in his voice.

He wanted to be there. He wanted to wrap a towel around his neck and take off for the waterfront. But no. He'd made other arrangements.

"I guess Miles caught you up on my summer plans?"

At that, the boys just nodded solemnly.

"Hey, Mack!" Miles took advantage of the awkward pause, elbowing his way to the camera. "How are you? How's ... Killington?"

"It's, uh ..." Mack searched for the right word. "It's fine." He swallowed hard as his friends looked skeptically at him through cyberspace. "Listen, I gotta run," he blurted, "but I just wanted to say Operation Extrication is off. Abort! Abort!"

While the rest of the assembled group shot each other

confused looks—Operation *what*?—Miles furrowed a brow at Mack.

"What do you mean?" he asked. "I was going to message you about that last night, but something ... happened."

"Really?" asked Mack, suddenly intrigued. "What's that?"

"That's THIS!" A large face invaded the screen. "That's ME! *I* happened!"

Mack saw the boy's crooked nose and immediately pegged him as the former pitcher of the Hortonia junior baseball team.

"Garth Fortin?!"

"Yeah, Garth here—" Miles started to explain.

"I told you last night! It's Forehead," Garth said, whipping a tennis ball at the wall as he walked away. "Call me Forehead."

"Miles!" Mack whisper-shouted. "What's going on?"

Miles shot an apologetic look at his friends, then carried the tablet into the bathroom stall at the back of the cabin and closed the door. Now only his face filled Mack's screen.

"You heard about the renovations at Hortonia, right?" He gave Mack the two-minute version of the story, right through the slap shot competition and Garth moving in.

Mack's eyes popped open. "He's in my bed?!" he shouted. "Him! Of all people!"

"If it makes you feel any better, we could say he's in Andre's," Miles offered. "That would mean a guy named Alexei Kozlov is in yours. He had Hortonia's second-best slap shot. Pat calls him *X* because he hasn't said a word."

"Well, that's something at least," Mack mused.

"But what's this about Operation Extrication? What's the prob—"

Miles was interrupted by a pounding at Mack's door.

"Breakfast, grunt!" croaked an adult male voice. "And don't forget your jacket!"

CHAPTER
4

"IT'S PROBABLY A BAD SIGN"

Miles heard his friend blurt a quick "Sorry, man, talk later," and watched the video chat window disappear from his screen. He opened the bathroom stall and walked through the cabin's lounge area, with its couch and little table, into the main room.

At that moment, Laker rolled over on his bed by the front door. "Not the short shorts," he mumbled in his sleep.

After a summer as camp baseball director, a plum job that came with its own living quarters, Laker had surprised everyone—especially Cheryl, the camp's longtime facilities administrator and new director—by taking a demotion and returning to life as a cabin counselor.

When he wasn't catching a few extra Zs before breakfast, he was telling anyone who asked that his solo cabin had had raccoons. But Miles suspected he had just missed his campers—until now.

"Keep it down, Laker!" Wi-Fi shouted, flailing his arm

out behind him and accidentally connecting with the counselor's mouth.

Wi-Fi, Nelson, Spike, and Mike could have played go fish anywhere, but they'd chosen the spot right next to Laker's bed.

"Wha—?!" shouted Laker, suddenly waking. "What is it?"

Wi-Fi shushed him angrily. "Somebody here's gotta have a queen. But I can't concentrate with all your talking."

"Ramos does!" Garth yelled as Laker groaned and covered his head with his pillow.

"Hey!" shouted Nelson.

"Nelson, do you have a queen?" Wi-Fi blurted.

The Triplett twins threw their cards down in unison.

"That's not …" Mike started.

"… fair!" Spike finished.

Suddenly, a small girl with dark hair and olive skin burst through the front door. "What's not fair?" shouted Nelson's little sister and frequent YouTube co-star.

"Cassie?!" Nelson shouted. "We've been over this! You're not allowed in the boys' cabins. What are you doing here?"

"Junior camp is so boring now," she said, squeezing in between Nelson and Wi-Fi to pick up the twins' cards from the floor. "Not even one person is fighting for the soul of this place."

Miles watched the melee from the back of the cabin, a small smile on his face.

Pat appeared from behind him. "Whoa, Miles," he said, holding his nose. Then to the rest of the group, he added, "You guys, do *not* go in there."

"Very funny, Pat." Miles stashed the tablet under Wi-Fi's pillow. "But the joke's on you. I didn't even go."

"Stopped up?" Pat asked, sounding concerned.

"No!" Miles reddened. "I was talking to Mack."

"About being stopped up?"

Miles grunted, realizing there was nothing he could say. He dropped onto his bed as the twins grabbed their cards back from Cassie and tried to resume the game.

Then Garth stood to face Pat in the center of the room. Pat looked around for a rescue but found none.

"So," Garth said, rocking back and forth on his heels, "gone on any good hikes lately?"

Now it was Pat's turn to blush. Two summers earlier, when he came to Mack's aid at the infamous camp social, Pat had made up a story about a secret peak on a hike the Hortonia kids were about to go on. Garth and his buddies took it as a challenge and ended up running through a patch of poison ivy. Afterward, everyone from Pat's campmates to his Hortonia rivals seemed to think he'd done it on purpose. But until now, he hadn't had to sleep in the same room as any of the Hortonians.

"Garth, I—"

"Forehead!" Garth said, cutting him off.

"But—"

"No buts!"

Pat had had enough. "Fine! Your name's Forehead. But I didn't do anything. I just made up some stuff to get you off Mack's back. I didn't know you'd walk through a bunch of poison ivy."

"Sure, I get it." Garth winked. "Like hockey legend Wayne Gretzky says, 'If at first you don't succeed, deny, deny again.' I respect that."

Miles's ears perked up. "That wasn't Wayne Gretzky. That was nobody."

Tired of the card game, Cassie walked over to sit at the edge of Miles's bed.

"You talked to Mack?" she asked him. "What'd he say?"

Laker looked up, loosening the grip on the pillow he'd used to cover his ears. "Wait … Cassie?! What are you doing here?"

"That's what I asked her," Nelson mumbled, forking over the two of spades to Spike.

"Out!" Laker shouted. "Nelson, walk your sister back to her cabin. Miles, you go with them so it looks like we're at least *trying* with the buddy-system rule. I'm not getting fired on the first day of camp!"

The term "buddy system" reminded Miles of his friends at Killington. Mack had often used the phrase to justify giving up his own summer to make Andre's a little better.

It also reminded Miles of Mack's favorite topic, which he'd brought up that morning: Operation Extrication, their plan to figure out how to get Andre out of Killington.

Miles's mind raced. Mack had said to call off the mission, which evidently meant he'd been compromised somehow. Maybe he was being watched too closely or had given up hope they'd be able to find the answer. But why did that mean *Miles* had to give up? He wanted—no, *needed*—to get his friends back to Camp Average, where they belonged.

But how would he pull it off? The pair could walk the distance between camps in an afternoon, but Andre had been very clear about wanting to honor his word and ride out the whole summer. Only the loophole of all loopholes could change that, and the problem hurt Miles's head whenever he devoted any time to it.

He could involve his friends at Camp Average, but ...

he didn't want to. While he was willing to acknowledge the fact that many heads are better than one, he didn't have to act on it.

No. This problem belonged to him.

"Bye, guys," Cassie shouted as she left the cabin. Then, in an exaggeratedly romantic voice, she added: "Bye, Pat."

As he followed the Ramos siblings out, Miles heard Pat smack his forehead.

"No, really—what did Mack say?" Cassie repeated her question once they'd got out the door. "How is it over there? How's Andre?"

Miles sighed as he took in the topography of senior camp. It was slightly more elevated than junior camp, and the ground was dryer, the pathways hard and weather-beaten.

"Mack didn't really get into it," he said. "Which could be a good sign … or a bad one."

Nelson and Cassie looked at him skeptically.

"Okay, fine," Miles said. "It's probably a bad sign."

CHAPTER
5

"THE *WHOLE* OUTFIELD?"

Mack and Andre stood with several others behind a chain-link backstop, watching a coach in a backward hat take batting practice from a live pitcher.

On leaving his room, Mack had found his schedule on a printout outside the door. As a member of the Mendoza dorm, he thought he'd be directed to a dusty backlot diamond to compete for grounders with stray dogs. But when he arrived at his appointed field—one of ten perfectly maintained diamonds that made Killington the camp look more like Killington the major-league training facility—he'd found Andre there. As newcomers of the same age, the two boys had the same schedule—a small, unexpected mercy.

While they watched the coach hit, Mack told Andre the story of his night and morning. Then Andre told him the story of his own.

"I … uh, don't have roommates," he finally blurted.

Mack whipped his head around. "What?!" he asked. "It sounded like you said you don't have roommates."

"I don't. But my room sounds like it might be bigger than yours. It's got a king-size bed and a walk-in closet and a couch and a private bathroom."

"Is that it?"

"Did I mention the fifty-inch TV? I fell asleep watching the A's game." Andre reflexively adjusted the brim of his green-and-yellow Oakland Athletics cap.

"No," Mack said flatly, "you didn't mention the fifty-inch TV."

Reo sidled up to them, his eyes firmly on the swing of the coach in the batter's box. "I *told* you that," he said to Mack. "Deets supposedly has an HD projector like the one in the clubhouse. He's going to hate to give it up when I prove I'm more deserving of it."

"Andre, meet Reo." Mack gestured to his roommate. "Reo, Andre."

"I know who he is," Reo admonished. "You don't hit a foul ball into the Camp Roundrock office without your name making the rounds." Then he held out his hand to Andre. "I'm an admirer, but you're my competition, too."

Andre shook it. "Fair enough."

Mack scratched his temple. "Am *I* your competition?" he asked playfully.

"Ha," Reo said, not laughing. "You're not even in my league."

Reo walked away while Andre chuckled. "That was pretty good," he said. "Credit where it's due."

Soon the coach in the batter's box raised his hand to stop the pitcher. He thrust his bat into a bag and turned to his new pupils. Only then did Mack realize the coach was his dorm supervisor. In this setting, he looked five years younger and at least as many times happier.

"My name is House," he said for the kids who hadn't had the pleasure of meeting him the night before. "I'll be one of your coaches this summer."

Suddenly Mack realized where he'd seen him before: House was the coach of the Killington junior team the year Camp Average had won the trophy. That explained why he was currently slumming it as supervisor of the worst dorm at camp. He was being punished.

House directed the players onto the field and had them introduce themselves. Mack heard someone cough and say "Hack!" when he said his name, but he figured it was just Reo and took no offense.

"Okay, let's get started with a little game of flip," House told them when the introductions were finished.

The boys arranged themselves into two loose circles of

ten players and began passing the ball back and forth—both catching and throwing it with their gloves.

Mack heard a tinny snippet of a punk rock song emerge from House's smartphone and watched the coach duck behind a nearby equipment shed. He got so distracted waiting for House to re-emerge that the ball hit him in the chest and dropped to the ground.

"Nice catch, man!" Andre jeered, drawing a few reluctant laughs from the group.

Mack picked the ball off the ground with the end of his glove and flipped it to Reo, starting the game anew.

Finally, House came out from behind the shed, a defeated look on his face. "Looking good, guys," he said. "Let's do some batting practice. Head over to the backstop."

Mack and Andre started to move with the group before House grabbed them each by the shoulder. "Not you two. You guys take the outfield."

Mack took in the expanse of clipped green grass extending from the left-field line to the right-field line. It might as well have been the Atlantic Ocean.

"The *whole* outfield?" he asked.

House had to look away. "Yeah. Catch what you can and shag the rest."

Mack opened his mouth for further protest, watching

as a massive amount of capable outfield help wandered toward the dugout, when Andre stopped him.

"You got it, Coach," he said. "We're on it."

Andre took off for right-center field, leaving left-center for Mack.

House set up on the mound and delivered a pitch to a waiting batter, who knocked it into right. Andre caught it on one hop and whipped it back into the infield.

The pitches and swings started to come faster and faster. Mack caught a pop fly, and Andre chased down a liner. Then the batter blasted a few to dead center, leaving the two boys to take turns chasing them to the fence.

Each hitter got five minutes at bat. By the third one, Mack and Andre were coated in sweat, and it only got worse from there.

Finally, House checked his watch and called for their turn.

The two friends loped slowly to the infield. Just then, a chime sounded across the field.

"This concludes the morning session," Maxwell said over the camp's loudspeakers. "Please proceed to your dorms to wash up, then head on to the clubhouse for lunch."

Mack threw his head back in frustration.

"Hey," said House, a guilty look on his face, "you guys'll get a chance. Trust me."

And they did. After lunch, Mack and Andre each got a shot at the plate. But House suddenly seemed unable to control his pitches, meaning the two boys got few balls to hit. They were also facing an outfield full of players, none of whom waited in the dugout.

As Andre left the box having barely touched the ball, the snickers rained down.

"Isn't that dude in the Ruth building?" said one kid in the infield.

"Not for long," said another.

The group spent the rest of the day bouncing between drills, from fielding to bunting to base running. Each time, Mack and Andre went last, if they went at all. And each time, the rest of the players delighted in pointing out flaws under their collective breath.

Eventually, Maxwell came over the loudspeaker again to announce dinner. Mack and Andre slumped down on the grass to catch their breath.

"If I didn't know any better," Andre said, "I'd say that day was planned by none other than Winston Smith."

Mack shook his head. *This place doesn't need a Winston*, he thought. *This place* is *Winston*.

CHAPTER
6

"HARD TO BEAT CHERRIES"

Miles stood on his toes in line for the mess-hall steam table, trying to peer around his cabinmates in front of him. When he got close enough to see it was pizza night, he turned abruptly by reflex.

"Hey, Mack, it's your—" Miles was suddenly nose to nose with a familiar face. Just not the familiar face he'd been expecting. "Favorite."

"How's it going, Miles?" asked Nicole. "How's Garth? How's the cabin?"

"It's fine," Miles lied, hearing Mack's voice come out of his mouth. He shuffled forward in line. "What about you? How are things going?"

Nicole wrinkled her nose and turned up the corner of her mouth.

"What?" Miles prodded.

"No Swish City this year. Not enough players, and not enough money for the entry fee."

Miles didn't need further explanation. Nicole was one of the best and most competitive athletes at camp, but since she'd arrived at Camp Average, her elite girls' teams hadn't found any nearby camps to take on.

The summer before, the co-ed Swish City 5-on-5 basketball tournament had fixed that problem. With Nicole as co-captain, Camp Average had made it all the way to the final against Camp Roundrock and earned the silver medal. Pat, whose affection for silver was as strong as it was strange, still wore the evidence under his shirt wherever he went.

Without that tournament, though, she was back at square one.

"Sorry, Nicole," Miles said, turning to collect a couple of veggie slices from the steam table. "I'm sure you'll—"

"Oh, don't worry about me," she said brightly. "I've already got a new sport."

Miles turned back, his brow furrowed in confusion, but she had already collected her pizza and was moving through the spare, high-ceilinged room to her cabin's table. "And let's just say it involves ma—"

A huge crash of pots and pans from the kitchen drowned out the end of her sentence.

New sport? Miles thought. *And did she say ... "mallards"?*

He decided to shake off the questions. He had enough on his mind.

47

By the time he got to his own table, everyone else from his cabin was already there—including Cassie, who was sharing her brother's chair as usual and somehow had already started on a bowl of cherries jubilee from the dessert station.

He slid into a seat between Wi-Fi and Pat, whose pizza sat uneaten in front of him as he stared across the table at Garth.

"Funny thing happened on my way to the pool after lunch," Pat said.

"You don't say," Garth replied, tearing a giant chunk of dough, cheese, and sauce off his slice.

"I *do* say," Pat continued. "When I pulled my swim shorts out of the dresser, they were lined with poison ivy leaves."

"Huh!" Garth said through pizza.

"There was poison ivy stuck to every other piece of my clothing, too."

"Weird."

Pat leaned forward. "That's all you've got to say?"

Miles watched in disgust as Garth held his greasy index finger against his nose, as if deep in thought.

"Hmm," he said. Then he scratched his head, rubbing the grease into his hair. "Yeah, I think that's it."

Pat stood and pointed a finger in Garth's face. "You did it, and you know it!"

"Did what?" Garth asked innocently, even as he was picking up a piece of pizza from Pat's plate.

"Confess!"

"I'm sure I don't know what you're talking about."

Pat pointed at Garth's hands, which were blotchy with pink-and-white patches. "You've got calamine lotion all over!" he shouted triumphantly. "You got poison ivy collecting all the leaves you stuffed into my undies!"

Garth wiggled his fingers. "Oh no," he said. "This is … oatmeal."

"It's dinnertime! You're eating pizza!"

"Well, then, it's steel-cut oats."

"That's just classy oatmeal!"

Laker pushed his plate to the middle of the table. "What are you yelling about now, Pat?"

Pat opened his mouth, but Garth cut him off, thrusting his hand toward Laker. "He gave me poison ivy! Again!"

Laker had been coaching Camp Average when the Hortonia baseball team was forced to bow out of the all-camp tournament two summers before. "Pat!" he shouted. "Seriously?"

"It wasn't me!"

Laker raised an eyebrow. "Yeah," he said, "name one other time that's been true."

Pat threw up his hands. "Okay, so I guess a really, really long track record can be used against someone now."

"Yes! It can!" Laker exclaimed. "Now let's go talk to Cheryl about what happens if you keep poisoning your roommates."

"Technically speaking," Miles offered, "the oil in poison ivy isn't poison. It's more like an irritant."

"So is Pat!" Laker said.

As Laker dragged Pat away, Wi-Fi suddenly jutted a finger into the air.

"Idea for a video game!" he declared. Since arriving at camp, he and Nelson had come up with dozens of ideas for games, movies, and YouTube shows. "It's called *Pat-Man*. It's basically *Pac-Man*, but it's about Pat collecting silver dollars."

Nelson lit up. "And he's being chased by poison ivy leaves instead of ghosts!"

"But what replaces the cherries?" Wi-Fi asked.

The two boys looked at the ceiling and rubbed their chins as they thought this over. Then a loud sound interrupted their musing.

BUUUUURRRRRRRRRP!

Nelson looked at his sister in horror.

"Hard to beat cherries," she said, dabbing at the bright red filling in the corners of her mouth with a napkin.

Miles watched Wi-Fi, Spike, and Mike dissolve into giggles. Alexei may as well have been a million miles away. And Garth … seemed to be thinking about something, a strange smirk on his face.

"You know what's not hard to beat?" Garth said finally, swiveling toward Cassie. "You. On the ball-hockey court."

Nelson's eyes bugged out. "What did you just—"

"I got this!" Cassie said, cutting her brother off.

She picked up her spoon and pointed it at Garth. Her mouth tightened and her nostrils flared. Miles had the distinct feeling of not wanting to be on the other side of the look, but Garth kept smiling.

"I was going to give you a free pass because you're new here," she said, "but since you brought it up."

Cassie turned to the rest of the table to describe her afternoon. "Because we have just the one ball-hockey court, organizers had to combine both camps' practice sessions, across ages and skill levels. So I wind up in a session with Garth here—"

"Forehead!"

"And he spends the entire time trash talking. 'This isn't the way you do this,' 'That isn't the way you do that.'"

"It wasn't," Garth confirmed.

Nelson seemed about to burst, but Cassie carried on as if she hadn't heard a thing.

"During the scrimmage, he starts throwing his body around, bumping the goalie off her spot every chance he gets—basically walking around like he owns the place."

Garth crossed his arms. "Well, I hadn't thought about it, but I kinda do."

"How do you figure?" asked Wi-Fi. "You don't even *go* to this camp."

"It's summertime. I go to Hortonia in the summer." He gleefully cracked his knuckles. "So this must be Hortonia."

"It's not," Cassie said firmly. "I've only been coming here a year, but that's long enough to learn rule number one."

"Is it 'We're number two'?" Nelson asked.

"No, that's rule number two," Wi-Fi said, grinning.

"Rule number one is you can be annoying on purpose as long as you're funny—just ask Pat," Cassie said. "But you can't be *mean*." She scooped up her tray and stood, seeming much taller than her four feet, ten inches. "I don't care if you think I stink at ball hockey. Just keep it to yourself."

Garth shrugged. "I'll see what I can do."

Miles let out a long breath. Crisis averted—for now. He just hoped things weren't going as badly for Mack and Andre at Killington.

CHAPTER
7

"I'M NOT IN THE LINEUP"

As he settled into life at Killington, Andre endured no end of glares and sideways glances. Nobody he encountered seemed to know he'd been invited to camp by the guy on the posters above their beds. Instead, he was treated like he'd come to take what was theirs.

But with Mack around for moral support, he found it easy to let it all roll off, and he simply waited—waited for the opportunity he knew was coming.

Of course, when it finally arrived, Andre was in the shower.

He had slept well in his giant bed and woken up with the sun, then headed to the shower in his private bathroom to wash off the dust, grime, and grass of a day at camp. Halfway through, he realized his tablet was pinging.

And pinging.

And pinging.

"I'm coming!" he shouted, leaving a trail of drips behind him as he ran into the room in a plush white robe.

He picked the tablet off his dresser and struggled to open it with soggy fingers. Finally succeeding, he pushed a button to cast its contents onto the room's TV.

Andre had received the same notification twelve times. It included a GIF of a fist-pumping baby, and it was adorned with two words in capital letters:

"GAME TODAY."

As Andre's stomach fluttered, he clicked through to his camp mail for the details. "Five-inning intra-camp game," the message said. "Thirteen-year-olds from Ruth and Mays (home team, in white) vs. Koufax, Dietrich, and Mendoza (away team, in gray). Main field. After dinner. Bring your game faces."

Andre bounded across the room with a series of karate chops and kicks. Then his arms fell to his sides as he realized that the game structure meant he'd be playing against Mack.

Oh, well, he thought with a sly grin. *He likes being number two.*

Andre floated through the day, more immune than ever to his campmates' scorn. He returned to his room after dinner, dressed in the bright white uniform with navy pinstripes he found in his closet, and sized himself up in the ornate full-length mirror at the end of his bed.

The effect was striking. His eyes seemed brighter, his cheekbones sharper, his shoulders broader. Andre felt like he could be heading out to the mound at Yankee Stadium to pitch in front of fifty thousand screaming fans. Apart from his Oakland A's cap, that is, which he had yanked on by habit. He reluctantly switched hats, pulling on the navy Killington one with "CK" stitched on the front. Then he grabbed his glove and bolted out the door.

Five minutes later, he emerged through a tunnel into the back door of the home dugout at Killington's main field. It might not have been Yankee Stadium, but it was close.

The dugouts were poured in concrete and set below field level, just like the ones in the majors. The grass was immaculately cut and the reddish-brown infield dirt immaculately raked, and the mostly empty green-painted stands stretched all the way down both foul lines. In the evening sun, the white bases and baselines shone so brightly they hurt Andre's eyes.

His cleats clacked against the dugout floor as he walked

through to find a place on the bench. Several teammates had arrived before him, but only one of them looked up.

"Looking good, Dre," said Deets.

Andre waited for the follow-up snipe, but it never came.

"Thanks," he said.

Soon, the Ruth and Mays players took the field to stretch, jog, and warm up their arms. As they returned to their home team dugout to check the newly posted lineup card, Andre saw Mack emerging from the visitors'.

"You're in trouble," Andre mouthed.

"Obviously," his friend shot back, smiling.

Andre ducked into the dugout, looking for his name in the third or fourth slot on the lineup card, where he'd always found it when playing for Camp Average or his team back home. But he didn't see it. He looked up and down and didn't see his name at all.

Until he looked at the area reserved for bench players.

There he was, right at the very bottom, buried beneath a handful of other benchwarmers. And his last name was misspelled: "Jeanings."

Andre felt like he'd swallowed a catcher's mitt. When he'd made the deal with Deets to spend his summer at Killington, he knew he'd miss his friends. But he figured at least he'd get to play baseball. It was his favorite sport, after all, and this was the perfect place to play it.

But what if they didn't let him play it at all?

While the starters poured out of the dugout, Andre sat down across from Deets, who was tightening the laces on his cleats.

"Um, Deets? Terry? I'm not in the lineup," he whispered, trying not to cause a scene.

"Huh," Deets replied loudly with an odd note of pride in his voice. "Weird."

He stood, picked up his extra-long glove, and cheerily clattered out of the dugout.

The game began a couple of minutes later, and Andre quickly got the sense that whoever had written his opponents' lineup card did it blindfolded. Or worse, like he didn't care at all.

First up were two big-swinging kids—classic cleanup hitters—who struck out in turn. Then Mack showed up in the three spot. The team's manager hadn't even bothered to factor in the grudge against Camp Average kids and leave him on the bench.

The first thing Andre noticed was how comfortable Mack looked. He reveled in making the pitcher wait a few extra seconds before he entered the box, tapping his aluminum bat against his heels.

When he finally did step in, he looked calm and confident, rolling his head on his shoulders as he sized up the pitcher. Andre realized this was no accident. Unlike everyone else at Killington, Mack had absolutely nothing to lose. He was on the lowest rung of the ladder and had no interest in climbing.

The outcome of this at-bat didn't matter—and that was immensely helping his game.

Mack patiently watched three balls pass outside the strike zone. He even watched a strike head down the pipe without lifting the bat off his shoulder.

Then the fifth pitch arrived, and Mack pounced. With his legs transferring a ton of force into his upper body, he uncoiled his long arms and swung hard through the zone.

PING!

He made perfect contact with the barrel of the bat, pulling the ball deep into the gap in left-center. As the outfielders chased it to the fence, Mack bolted out of the box, rounded first base, and slowed to a trot at second, stopping there with a stand-up double.

His teammates jumped and cheered, drawing life from the surprise hit, and Andre subtly pumped his fist on the bench. "Power bat," he whispered, quoting his friend.

The next batter, Reo, came through with a single to bring Mack home for the first run of the game, but the rally ended there.

In the bottom half of the inning, Andre watched

helplessly as his teammates evened up the score. Then he watched them go ahead by a run in the second. But they didn't pull away. Not even Deets, who struck out and popped out in his first two at bats, could make anything happen for his team.

By the top of the fifth and final inning, they were still up just one run. Maxwell, the manager for Andre's team, subbed in his third pitcher of the game (who gave up a single), then immediately went to his fourth (who gave up a walk).

Maxwell tore off his cap and hit his leg with it, no longer the saintly presence he'd been in the clubhouse on the first night of camp. No matter how high he'd risen at Camp Killington, he was still a victim of the place he'd helped create—a place where losing was not an option.

He tossed his cap on the bench and grabbed the lineup card. He ran his finger down the page until he reached the last name on it.

"Jeanings!" he shouted.

Andre stood at light speed. "It's Jennings," he corrected.

"Whatever. You're our only pitcher left," Maxwell said, choking on his words. "If this batter gets on, you're in. Start warming up."

Andre's eyes narrowed. He grabbed the team's backup catcher, a skinny boy named Brandon, and walked out of the dugout as the next batter approached the plate. It was Mack.

The two nodded at each other with serious but encouraging looks on their faces.

Come on, man, Andre thought. *Get on base so I can take you out.*

Andre turned and headed to the makeshift bullpen in left-field foul territory. He and his catcher tossed the ball back and forth a few times, then Brandon got into a crouch, pulled on his mask, and called for a fastball.

"Let's see what you got, Jeanings."

Andre shut the world out, forgetting even to check Mack's progress at the plate. He wound up and fired a fastball that nearly tore through Brandon's mitt.

"Yow!" the catcher grunted.

Brandon called for another fastball. Then a changeup. Then a curve. Each flew in for what would obviously be strikes.

He was warm. He was ready.

"Attaboy, Mack!" Andre heard someone shout.

"Time!" Maxwell called as Mack trotted to first base, the recipient of another free pass.

As the coach walked to the mound, he looked to the bullpen and patted his left arm. He wanted the leftie. He wanted Andre.

"Don't screw this up," Brandon said.

Andre ran to the mound, where Maxwell and all the infielders—including Deets—were waiting for him.

"Bases juiced, nobody out. But you got this." Maxwell sighed as he handed Andre the ball. At a camp like this, it might as well have been his hard-earned reputation.

The coach walked off toward the dugout. Andre stood tall as the gathered infielders tapped his arms with their gloves and likewise dispersed.

Alone on his mound island, he took in the full task ahead. He knew he had the stuff to strike out three players in a row, but he also knew a fluke bloop single could score two runs. So he faced the catcher, watched third base out of the corner of his eye, and patiently waited for the runner there to lead off. Lead-offs weren't allowed in twelve-and-under play, but Andre knew they were fair game—and basically irresistible—now that the boys were thirteen.

When the runner took a few steps down the line, Andre spun quickly and whipped a strike to the cleats of his teammate at third base, a boy named Simi, who simply had to catch the ball to tag out the runner as he slid back to the base.

"One down!" Maxwell shouted. "Nice play, Jeanings!"

Before Andre could say anything, Simi called out, "It's *Jennings!*"

"All right, fine! *Jennings!*" the coach said, sounding hurt. "Let's mow 'em down, Jennings."

But Andre had other ideas. He'd spent so much time watching his opponents, he knew what was coming next.

He bent low, looking for his sign.

The catcher put one finger down. Fastball.

Andre shook his head.

The catcher put two fingers down. Curveball.

Andre shook his head.

The catcher put down four fingers. Changeup.

Again, Andre shook his head.

The catcher called time and ran out to the mound.

"What's the deal, man?" he asked from behind his glove. "You don't have any pitches left."

"Pitch-out."

"What?!"

But Andre meant it. He wanted to pitch high and way outside on purpose.

"The guy on second is the most aggressive kid on the field. They're going to try for the double steal."

The catcher thought about it. "If you say so," he said.

He called Simi over from third base, and from the outside looking in, it may have seemed he was looking for support in convincing Andre to take his signs.

"Sometime this month," Deets called from first base.

After a quick scrum, the fielders returned to their positions.

Andre went into his windup, and both base runners took off as soon as the ball left his hand. The catcher caught the ball standing up and fired it to Simi, who easily tagged out his second runner of the inning.

Mack got in safely to second, but with two out and just one on, Andre finally decided he could focus on the actual batter.

And he struck him out on three straight pitches.

Three down. Game over.

"Yeah!" shouted Maxwell.

"That's how it's done!" yelled Brandon from the dugout, jumping to his feet and cheering at the one-player show Andre had put on. "Apparently!"

As Andre walked to the dugout in the waning light of the day, a huge smile crept over his face. It only got larger as his teammates raced by him, high-fiving and chittering all the way.

"You were right," Andre heard Simi whisper to their team's shortstop. "Dude can play."

The shortstop nodded. "And you haven't even seen him hit."

CHAPTER
8

"LOOK ALIVE, JONES!"

Mack jogged in from second base, a flare of happiness in his gut despite the loss. It hadn't been easy watching Andre sit in the dugout all game like a caged falcon, but now—after one five-minute display of greatness—the coaches would be crazy to stick him there again.

As he went to collect his hat and glove, Mack watched two infielders hovering around Andre like they wanted to ask for autographs—but something held both of them back from actually talking to him.

Then Mack noticed something else and stopped short.

Deets slipped into the dugout and threw his glove into the wall, where it squashed like a tomato and slumped to the ground. He left it where it lay—suddenly somebody else's job to pick up—and stomped the length of the dugout, disappearing out the back.

Mack didn't know why Andre had been left off his team's lineup card, or what Deets thought about the decision. But he knew Deets had wanted Andre here for a reason, and suddenly that reason didn't seem to be helping the team win. Their team *had* won. But the big man on camp sure wasn't celebrating.

And so, neither could Mack—no matter how proud of his friend he was.

He had a strong urge to follow Deets. Where was he going so fast? Who was he going to talk to? But Mack didn't get a chance.

"Nice game," said Reo, thrusting out a hand as Mack reached his own dugout. "You're not nearly as bad as I thought you'd be."

Mack warily offered his hand.

"A couple of hours of film study a night, and you might even fix that hitch in your swing."

Mack shot the boy a mocking grin. "Thanks," he said sarcastically, things returning to normal between them.

Then Benny appeared. "Nice game," he said, echoing their roommate. "Period. Full stop."

"You, too," Mack replied. Benny hadn't got on base, but he had played flawlessly at catcher.

The three of them left the field. As they walked in silence to their dorm to get ready for lights-out, Mack forgot all about Deets and felt a sudden calmness come over him.

Things could be worse, he thought.

"Look alive, Jones!"

From the comfort of his bed, Mack heard a pounding noise and groggily tried to make sense of it. Judging by the almost perfect darkness of the room, he guessed it was nowhere near morning. He felt a twinge of pity for this "Jones" person before rolling onto his back and pulling the covers to his chin.

Then he pulled them down again and opened his eyes.

Wait, he thought. *That's me.*

Mack sat up quickly, bashing his head on the underside of the top bunk. He stumbled to the door, wincing and rubbing his head the whole way.

"What is it?" he asked, pulling open the door.

On the other side he found House, bathed in cold halogen light from the hallway. He was holding a thermos of coffee, but the dark bags under his eyes looked full of hockey equipment.

"About time," he snarled. "Let's go."

"Go where?" Mack said, still rubbing his head.

"Rookie orientation."

Mack looked skeptically at House. He didn't want to drag his fellow rookie roommates into this, but he was too curious not to ask. He jerked a thumb back into his darkened room. "What about them?"

"Rookie orientation for guys with your name," deadpanned House, checking his smartwatch.

"That hardly seems—"

"Please, Mack!" Reo moaned. "Make your principled stand somewhere else!"

Mack slumped. He glanced up at the bunk above his and saw Benny lying facedown with his pillow wrapped around his head. He realized that fighting this—whatever it was—was only going to punish his roommates.

"What time is it?" he asked quietly.

"Don't ask. In fact, don't ask anything else at all." House took a big swig of his coffee. "Just get dressed. And don't bother bringing your glove."

Mack looked at the dorm supervisor with suspicion. "Fine."

He closed the door to shut out the hallway light. While tugging on his socks, he stumbled sideways and nearly landed on an open tablet lying on the floor.

Reo had stayed up late—again—going over every millisecond of the footage he'd been sent of his at bats during the intra-squad game. Mack had fallen asleep to him muttering to the version of himself on the screen, "Quit dropping your back elbow. What is this, T-ball?"

Mack picked up the tablet and placed it on Reo's dresser, triggering the motion sensor in the process. The screen's clock told him it was just after 1:00 a.m.

When he emerged into the hallway a minute later, he found it empty, so he continued outside. There, he found a thick cloud cover, no moon, and a light, warm drizzle in the air. In the distance, he saw House opening the door of the Ruth building.

"Andre," Mack said aloud. "Of course."

By the time he'd reached the building, House was already on his way back out.

"Hurry up," he said into the darkness behind him. "We're late."

Andre emerged, rubbing his eyes as he crossed the threshold. "Late for *what*?" he asked.

House shook his head. "Trust me when I say you don't want to know."

The dorm supervisor walked off toward the clubhouse. The boys shared a quick glance.

"Just us, huh?" Andre whispered.

"Looks like."

Reluctantly, the boys followed House along the winding path through the woods, then skirted the clubhouse and walked out into uncharted territory.

The non-baseball portion of the campus.

Mack and Andre had long heard the rumors about the other side of camp. The *other* Killington was supposed to be something like a country club, where campers split their days between leisure sports and spa treatments. There was even a story about a pool filled day and night with green smoothie.

"Are we even *allowed* on the country club side?" Andre whispered. "I feel like an alarm's going to go off."

The trio crested a low hill, passed between some tightly packed shrubs, and walked down the other side. Even in the dead of night, it was like descending a frozen mountainside to emerge in a tropical valley. The grounds on this side of the camp were even more green, even better kept, even more lavish. They were also twice as large. Mack noticed it had stopped raining, too, as if on cue.

In the soft light from several strategically placed antique street lamps, Mack counted six tennis courts, two in each surface—blue hard court, red clay, and green grass.

But none of those was their destination.

"House," Mack whined, "where are we going?"

House stopped abruptly, and the boys bumped into his back. "We're here," he said.

Mack and Andre collected themselves, then looked around. They were standing next to a kind of small football field, but without the lines. They could differentiate it from the rest of the beautifully kept lawn only by the length of the grass—which couldn't have been more than a half-inch.

"Where's here?" Mack asked.

House scoffed. "Haven't you seen a croquet pitch before?"

For a few seconds, Mack and Andre stared at the dorm supervisor.

"Excuse me?" Andre finally asked. "Is that some kind of bird?"

"A croquet pitch!" House seethed. "Croquet! The game with the colored balls and wooden mallets."

Mack knew the game House was talking about. He remembered playing it with his cousins when he was younger. But in his recollection, it was played on uneven backyard grass, and it usually ended in arguments over the rules and a search for balls in the bushes.

"You're saying there's a regulation field for that?"

"And it looks like *this*?" Andre followed up.

"Well, not really," House said. "This grass is too long. It's supposed to be exactly five millimeters high."

"Huh," Mack said, taking in what he thought was a random bit of trivia.

But House continued to stare at them.

"And?" Andre asked.

"And you guys are going to mow it."

"Us?!" Andre shouted. "Why us?!"

"Shh!" House cringed at Andre's volume and looked around. "It's a rookie tradition."

"Yeah, right," Mack said. "Rookie tradition *for guys with our names.*"

"Just stay here," House grunted. "I'll be right back."

The boys watched the dorm supervisor jog to a small shed nearby. It was tucked away near a stand of bushes, and the boys hadn't even noticed it. Mack guessed that was the point.

House dragged a push mower out of the shed, lifted it off the ground, and lugged it back to the pitch, setting it in the nearest corner.

"Okay." House wiped his brow with his sleeve. "Better get started."

Mack and Andre looked at each other in the darkness. On one hand, Mack thought, this was seriously uncool. They were being singled out because of where they used to go to camp. On the other hand, they'd seen worse punishments with less definite end points.

Andre seemed to read Mack's mind. "Fine," he told House, stepping behind the mower and pushing it forward.

For a second, watching the grass clippings shoot off the whirring blades into the attached tray, Andre seemed almost pleased with himself. Then Mack saw him look up and scan the pitch again. At that moment, it might as well have been a golf course. There was so much work ahead of them.

Andre slumped his shoulders and dropped his head, trudging down one long edge as Mack followed, waiting to tag in.

When Andre got to the corner of the pitch, he made a round turn and continued along the far edge. Just as Mack was about to offer to take over, he felt a hand on his shoulder.

"Here," said House, holding out a pair of scissors.

"What?" Mack grabbed at the collar of his new Killington T-shirt. "Is my tag sticking out?"

"No." House pointed at the corner of the pitch, where the mower had left a triangular patch uncut.

"What do you want me to do about that?"

Again, House held out the scissors.

Mack's eyes bugged out. "You want me to give the field a haircut?!"

House shrugged. "Whatever you want to call it."

"But," Mack protested, "we can just go over the corners again when we're done!"

"Nah, the scissors do a better job." He scratched the back of his head with the hand not holding the scissors. "And they're more efficient."

Mack was pretty sure House didn't know the meaning of the word. He suddenly wished Miles were there to offer a definition. Failing that, he had an urge to give House a few words of his own.

But as he watched Andre push the mower down the other long edge of the pitch, he decided to follow his lead.

Mack snatched the scissors from House's hand and went to work in the corner. Hunched over on his hands and knees, he trimmed the grass to the same height as the stuff Andre was leaving in his wake.

When he was done with the first corner, he ran to the next nearest one. By the time he'd finished the last of them, Andre was just wrapping up with the mower. Mack and House met him in the middle of the pitch.

"That wasn't so bad," Andre said, wiping the sweat from his brow with the bottom of his T-shirt.

House clucked his tongue, then pulled a ruler from his pocket and knelt to measure the height of the grass.

"Six millimeters," he said woodenly, as if reading from a script. He checked his phone—seemingly for instructions—and adjusted a lever on the lawn mower. "Once more around the pitch should do it."

Andre and Mack groaned.

The pair repeated their movements from the first time they'd completed the task, cutting precisely one more millimeter from the top of each blade of grass on the pitch. Then House measured again.

"Five millimeters exactly," he said with a thankful tone.

He placed the mower back where he had found it and ushered the boys in the direction of their dorms. As they went, Mack noticed him looking around the whole time, as if he was leaving the scene of a crime.

Within minutes, Mack was back at his dorm room, carefully opening the door so it wouldn't bash against Reo's bed.

He had just laid his head down on his pillow when he heard something.

His tablet was ringing.

"ARE YOU GOING TO GET THAT?!" moaned Reo.

Mack fumbled under his bed and pulled out his tablet. It was a video call. From Miles.

Mack reluctantly rose, stepped out into the hallway, and slumped down against the wall. Then he accepted the call.

CHAPTER
9

"I FAILED"

Miles watched Mack's face pop up on the tablet screen. "Oh, good!" he whispered gratefully. "You're up."

"Miles?" Mack asked. "What's going on? It's 3:00 a.m., and I'm exhausted. I just spent my night trimming a croquet pitch with a pair of scissors."

Miles recoiled. "A what with a what?!"

"Don't ask," Mack said. "What's up?"

Miles removed his glasses and cleaned them with the bottom of his orange camp T-shirt. He had tried to borrow Wi-Fi's tablet several times during daylight hours, but the cabin's tech wizard and Nelson had been using it all day—for what purpose, he couldn't tell. They mainly seemed to hold it aloft and talk to it with giddy looks on their faces, like it was a newborn baby. After lights-out, Miles had tossed and turned for hours before finally grabbing the tablet from its hiding place and sneaking into the bathroom stall.

"I couldn't sleep," he admitted. "I've been over it a million times, and I ... I failed."

"Failed?" Mack asked. "Failed what?"

"To get you out of Killington."

Miles listed off the options he'd thought up.

"I wondered if you could just disappear in the middle of the night, but that would work only until people noticed you were missing, and besides, I knew Andre wouldn't go for it," he said. "You could try tanking games or breaking rules to get kicked out, but again, Andre wouldn't be interested— and in the worst-case scenario, you might end up in more trouble with your parents than you could explain away."

Mack's face glowed in the tablet-screen light as he listened, but he said nothing. It was clear he'd been through these options on his own.

"I read every word of an online forum dedicated to legal loopholes and contractual deal breakers," Miles continued, "but none of them applied to a deal someone still wants to honor."

Miles looked away from the tablet. "I even emailed a town clerk's office to find out who owns Killington. I thought maybe I'd find something to get it shut down."

"What?!" Mack gasped, sounding both shocked and at least a little impressed.

"But I ditched that plan," Miles said softly. "And I never

heard back anyway. I just can't get you out of there. Not without creating new problems for you or hurting other people."

Mack smiled sadly. "It's okay, Miles. I never expected you to," he said. "Don't worry about it."

Fat chance, Miles thought gloomily.

Mack shook his head, then put on a brave face. "Hey," he said, changing the subject, "I haven't even told you about the intra-camp game yet. Andre killed it. You should've seen Deets's face. I thought he was going to put his fist through a wall."

Miles furrowed his brow. He could practically feel Mack's words pushing their way through his frontal lobe. He pulled back until his face was barely visible in the small window on his tablet screen.

"Deets was angry?" he asked slowly.

"That's an understatement," Mack replied.

"But weren't they on the same team?"

"They were," Mack said slowly, suddenly confused. "What is it?"

"I don't know yet." Miles's expression morphed into one of determination. He leaned back into the camera. "But I will."

჻

Miles finally fell asleep with Mack's words still rattling

around in his head. There was an idea there—something he hadn't thought of. Hadn't considered.

But he didn't get to sleep long.

"Back!" he heard Pat shout. "Stay back!"

Miles opened his eyes to find morning sunlight pouring in through the windows. Pat was standing on his bed and pointing his goalie stick at Garth, who was walking by with his hands in the air.

"I was just using the bathroom," he said, a smug smile on his face.

"I'll believe it when I smell it," Pat said, not taking his eyes off his enemy.

"Pat! Gross!" Miles yelled. "Let it go!"

"Fine," he told Miles, setting the goalie stick down as Garth picked up a hockey magazine and lay on his bed. "Just do me a favor."

"What's that?"

"Come to ball-hockey practice?" he whispered.

Miles suddenly got the feeling they were being watched. But he shook it off to shoot Pat a confused look. "Why?" he asked. "I don't even play ball hockey."

"I don't need you to play," Pat answered, still whispering. "I just need you to keep an eye on Garth."

"Forehead!" Garth shouted from the other side of the room.

"I'm worried he's going to mess with my gear while my back's turned."

Miles considered. As he had several times already that summer, he asked himself, *What would Mack do?* Then he dialed back the answer to something less drastic.

"Sure," he said. He was too distracted to have much fun at morning rocketry anyway. "I'll come. *To watch.*"

Pat pumped his fist. Then Miles headed to the sink to wash his face, only to find Nelson and Wi-Fi kneeling on the ground nearby, whispering into Wi-Fi's tablet.

Miles squinted. "What are you guys doing?"

Both boys jumped, and Wi-Fi reached for the tablet with shaky hands, poking at the screen.

"Tell me!" Miles pressed.

But before either boy could answer, a soccer ball flew by Miles's head and bounced off the back wall.

"Keep it …" yelled Mike, half out of his lower bunk at the front of the room.

"… down!" followed Spike.

"Some of us …"

"… are trying to sleep!"

Laker passed through the room, a towel over his shoulder, stealing Miles's place at the sink and scattering kids to their bunks. "Those two will make fine counselors one day," he said proudly.

Forty-five minutes later, the boys of cabin 23 had gone to morning flag-raising and finished breakfast, and Miles and Pat had been to the camp office to change Miles's morning schedule.

The sky was overcast, and the air was thick and warm as the pair walked past the senior cabins and skirted the pool to reach the ball-hockey court. On the way, they passed Nicole and Makayla walking in the opposite direction. Both girls were dressed all in white, and they were so deep in conversation they didn't even notice their friends.

"It itches!" Makayla tugged at the collar of her sleeveless V-neck sweater.

"What do you want me to do?" Nicole snapped as they trudged out of listening range. "It's a requirement!"

When Miles and Pat arrived at the ball-hockey court, twenty other kids were already there. The court itself was one of the newest things at Camp Average, and it stood out starkly from the green grass and oak trees around it. It was full-size—Miles guessed about two hundred feet long and eighty across—with three-foot-high white plastic boards all the way around. At the end of the court and in the corners, yellow netting sprang up from the boards to keep the ball from getting lost on wild shots. Along one side was a set of bleachers that sat maybe a hundred people.

The playing surface had a red-and-white line down the middle, a blue line halfway into either end, and a red line running along each net. There were red face-off circles at center court and near each of the corners.

"Okay," Pat said, holding out his fist for Miles to bump. "You got me?"

Miles reached out and grabbed Pat's fist. "You got it."

Pat shook his head and split off to find his gear. Miles leaned up against the boards at center court and watched the players move about like flies in a Mason jar.

"Hey, Miles!" shouted Cassie, running toward him.

She stopped abruptly about ten feet away, a bright orange ball seemingly stuck to her stick.

"How's it going?" she asked.

Before he could answer, she wound up and shot the ball directly at him. Miles froze, steeling himself for the impact of the ball, but it bounced off the boards—*SMACK!*—and ricocheted back to her.

"What are you up to?"

Again Miles opened his mouth to answer, and again Cassie shot the ball.

SMACK!

"Cassie!" Miles shouted, his heart racing.

"Yeah?" she asked, moving the ball back and forth along the ground with the blade of her stick.

"Quit it with the slap shots!" Miles shouted.

"Okay," she said, stopping the ball under her foot.

Miles took a relieved breath, then explained his presence at the court.

"I don't know what Pat's worried about," Cassie said when Miles had finished. "*I'm* the one who's really in trouble here."

"How do you mean?"

"Pat plays net! He doesn't have to deal with Garth out on the court."

Miles shrugged. He wasn't anybody's definition of a ball-hockey fan and didn't really know what she meant.

"If you could keep an eye out for me, too," Cassie continued, "that would be great."

Miles slumped a little, feeling a kind of weight on his entire body. Was there anyone else who wanted something from him? At least, he thought, this request required him to do no more than he was already doing—keeping an eye on Garth.

Who, Miles noticed suddenly, was about to steamroll Cassie from behind.

"Cassie, look—!" he started to shout.

But it was too late. Garth bumped shoulders with Cassie

as he popped the ball out from under her foot with his stick, bounced it off the boards to himself, and took off with it.

"Nice start, Miles!" Cassie yelled as she pitched to the side. Then she regained her balance, turned, and ran off. "Garth!"

"FOREHEAD!"

"That's *my* ball!"

This morning wasn't going the way Miles had planned. While keeping his eyes on Garth as he'd been asked to do, he tried to devote his conscious mind to his other problem. What had Mack said, and how did it change things?

But as full-face cage helmets went on and stick-and-ball drills began, Miles was even less able to focus on his conversation with Mack. Instead, he found himself watching Garth for reasons other than protecting his friends. If possible, he was even more natural with the ball on his stick than Cassie was.

Miles's newest cabinmate could fire shots with just a flick of his wrist. He could stab his stick at other players' feet and steal the ball without making contact. He could pass directly to the blades of his teammates' sticks, whether they were standing or on the move.

He was as good at ball hockey as he was at getting under people's skin.

Miles watched the players break into lines to take

penalty shots on Pat, who had suited up—no poison ivy in his gear, thankfully—to play in net. A seasoned goaltender, Pat could stop most of what came at him. But Garth's turns were a different story.

On his first attempt, he ran down, faked a slap shot, and squirted a wrist shot through Pat's legs.

On his second, he again faked a slap shot, then went to his back hand. And scored.

On his third, he simply rocketed the slap shot into the top corner of the net. Expecting a fake, Pat barely moved as the ball ripped past him, knocking his plastic water bottle to the ground.

"Let's take a break!" the coach yelled.

Pat collected his bottle and walked over to Miles. "Man," he said, shooting a stream of water through his face cage. "I want that guy *gone*."

Fireworks went off in Miles's brain. *Gone*. Pat wanted Garth to leave camp. Not because he was annoying. Not because he was at this very moment figuring out how to separate Pat from his shoes so he could stuff poison ivy into them.

But because he was *good*.

Miles leapt over the boards to give Pat a bear hug.

"Whoa!" his friend yelled, looking around uncomfortably. "There's no hugging in ball hockey."

"Not true," said Cassie, wrapping her arms around both boys. "You made that up."

"Doesn't matter either way!" Miles said. "I don't play ball hockey." He freed himself from Cassie's embrace, jumped back over the boards, and took off at a sprint.

"Hey!" Pat shouted after him.

"Where are you going?" Cassie chimed in.

Miles waved without looking back. "I have to make a call!"

CHAPTER
10

"WHAT HAVE WE
GOT TO LOSE?"

Mack followed Andre to the front door of the Ruth building, feeling out of place. The cobblestone path was nicer than the floors in his dorm.

"What's this about, anyway?" Andre asked as he led the way inside.

"I don't know." Mack pointed at the tablet under his arm. "Miles just said he'd call again after dinner and asked me to make sure you were there. I figured your room was a better venue than mine."

Secretly, Mack had suggested Andre's room because he wanted to know just how jealous he should be. The pair walked down the hallway, and Andre entered a room marked 1B—every room in the building had the number one on its door.

Mack followed, crossing the threshold with an involuntary whistle. The room was easily four times the size of his own—which, he couldn't help noting, had to hold three times as many people. The furniture looked far more comfortable, and there was far more of it.

"I'd invite you to stay here with me," Andre said as Mack studied the room in awe, "but—"

"We're trying to fit in. I get it."

Mack popped his head into the bathroom, eyeing the gleaming floors and fixtures. The clawfoot porcelain tub alone was bigger than his bed.

"If Miles doesn't call soon, though, could I take a shower?" he asked. "The lineup for the one on my floor is always ten guys long."

But Mack's tablet started buzzing before Andre could answer. He set it up on the dresser and accepted the call.

"Miles?" Mack asked as his friend's image came on the screen. He seemed to be in a wooden sound booth. "Where are you?"

"Lodge bathroom. Everyone else is watching a movie," he said. "And probably a little bit worried that I have irritable bowel syndrome."

Andre pulled up two chairs, and he and Mack appeared in the small inset box on the screen.

"Andre!" Miles shouted.

"Hey, Miles. How's camp?"

Miles shrugged. "Not the same without you."

"I heard it's not the same for other reasons, too. How are the Hortonia guys fitting in?"

"Terribly," Miles said in a surprisingly upbeat voice. "But that's not why I wanted to talk to you."

"So lay it on us."

Miles took a breath. "I thought of a way to get you out," he said quickly.

Andre shook his head. "Sorry? A way to get us out … of *here*?"

"Precisely."

Mack watched Andre's shoulders drop.

"Miles, man," he said consolingly, "I appreciate it. I really do. And you know I'd rather spend my summer at Camp Average."

"But … ?" Miles began.

"But I'm at Killington because I'm holding up my end of a deal. And Mack's at Killington because …" Andre trailed off, glancing over at his friend. "Because he's weird?"

"Hey!" Mack batted Andre lightly on the shoulder. "Maybe you'd like to tend that croquet pitch by yourself next time."

"The croquet pitch! Thanks for bringing that up." Miles narrowed his eyes. "Who do you think made you do that? Was it the camp director?"

Andre twisted his mouth in thought. "He barely seems to know our names."

"Or this House guy?"

Mack remembered the dorm supervisor's obvious discomfort during their midnight landscaping mission. "No," he said. "I don't think so."

"So who, then?"

Mack and Andre frowned, thinking.

"I'll give you a hint," Miles said. "His name starts with a *D* and rhymes with 'eats.'"

Andre scoffed. "Come on."

"I'm serious," Miles said, his face grim. "It was Deets who kept you both up all night mowing that croquet pitch. It was Deets who stuck Mack in the Mendoza building and got you left off the lineup card. He's messing with you. Just like Winston would if he were there."

Andre's skeptical look remained. "Winston was trying to make us better so he could look good. But why would Deets want to mess with us? He has nothing to gain. Unless …"

"Unless he's not trying to gain anything," Miles said, finishing Andre's thought. "He's just trying to get back at you."

Mack had a moment of realization. "Miles is right!" he said, connecting the dots in his head. "Deets is working from Winston's playbook!"

"But …" Andre tried to head his friend off, but it was like trying to stop a runaway freight train.

"He even found himself a Laker to carry out his orders," Mack continued, referring to their old cabin counselor, who was forced to do Winston's bidding in his first summer at camp. "That's why House is acting so weird!"

Andre scratched his chin, still unconvinced. "But if this is Winston 2.0, then I know what you're going to say next."

"I don't think you do," Miles replied.

"I'm not going to play badly on purpose."

"And I don't think you should."

Mack and Andre both shook their heads. "Huh?" they asked in unison.

"Deets may be just as underhanded as Winston, but he wants the opposite of what Winston wanted. He wants you to give up, to break your spirits—he wants you to play badly. So to handle Deets, you should do the opposite of what we did with Winston."

"Excuse me?" Andre said.

"You should *win* so much that Deets gets you kicked out. You should be yourselves. Don't try to blend in."

Mack did a double take. This was a new one.

"Think about it," Miles explained. "Deets is a legend

around that place, but we already got the better of him once. Now he's trying to protect his legacy—by ruining Andre's."

Mack and Andre frowned in confusion.

"He's *jealous* of you, Andre. He thought if he could get you into his arena, he could control you like he does everything else there. But if he discovers he can't, then— maybe—he'll send you home."

Andre's chest heaved as his breaths came in short bursts. "How could he do that? He's just a kid!"

"If he can fix dorm assignments and keep a counselor under his thumb, he can figure it out," Miles insisted. "Heck, he even organized a bus for us last summer. Like him or not, he has pull at that place."

Mack waited for Andre's next question, but it didn't come. He searched and found nothing in his friend's blank expression.

Finally, after an incredibly long ten seconds, Andre shrugged his shoulders. "What have we got to lose?" he asked.

CHAPTER
11

"LET'S GET IT"

The next morning, the sound of baseball meeting aluminum rang out before dawn.

PING.

PING.

PING.

Rubbing his eyes in the cool morning air, House yanked open the door of the camp's batting cages and stomped down to the third and final cage. Andre stood at the plate while Mack fed a neon blue Jugs BP3 pitching machine. A ball shot through the machine and down the pipe.

PING!

"What are you guys doing in here?!" House screamed.

Mack and Andre froze in place, turning their heads to look at him. A ball zipped by Andre, who was locked in his batting stance, and slammed into the thick plastic curtain at the back of the cage with a smack.

"Laundry?" Andre answered finally.

"Times tables!" Mack shouted from the pitching machine, cupping a hand around his mouth.

SMACK.

"Mack!" House shouted in exasperation. "Stop feeding balls."

SMACK.

"What?" Mack shouted back.

"Stop it!" House bellowed. "Get out of here!"

SMACK.

Mack hit a button on the back of the pitching machine, and it whirred to a stop.

"No problem!" Andre said, wrapping a white towel around his neck and exiting the cage. "We only wanted to put in an hour anyway."

The two left House behind to jog through the sleeping camp to the clubhouse, which wasn't yet open for its daily business. After the boys had spent a few minutes peering through the glass double doors, though, the bleary-eyed chefs took pity on them, delivering small paper sacks of fruit and buns and hard-boiled eggs with plastic bottles of orange juice.

Mack and Andre ate in the visitors' dugout at their usual practice field, calmly munching away as the sprinklers finished their nightly routine and disappeared underground.

They stretched and jogged around the field for thirty minutes. Then they went through the long-toss routine Mack had found online, moving farther apart from each other as they went along, surprising themselves with the distance they could get when they put backspin on the ball and added a little hop before each throw. When their usual practice mates arrived, they were standing over 150 feet apart, heaving the ball back and forth on a high arc.

"Sweet," breathed Benny.

House busted into the scene with a grunt. "Okay," he shouted impatiently. "Let's do a little batting practice. Just not—"

"Mack and Andre!" Mack yelled out, finishing the coach's sentence.

Benny watched Mack and Andre race to opposite fields as they had on the first day of practice. Then he ran after them.

"Benny!" House shouted. "Where are you going?"

"Center field!"

Mack and Andre gave him air fist bumps from their respective zones as they veered closer to the foul lines to cover more ground.

"Ready!" Mack shouted toward the infield.

But before a fuming House could throw a single pitch to the first batter, the punk rock ringtone of his smartphone went off. Mack and Andre knew now—beyond any doubt—what that ringtone meant. It was Deets, and House reacted to the sound like it was an alarm clock on the day of a big exam.

The coach let out a sigh heard around the field. "Andre!" he shouted finally. "Come pitch."

As House walked off toward the equipment shed, Andre pumped his fist, then ran to the mound and stretched out his arm.

"Okay, fine," said Reo from the bench, responding to a request no one had made. "I'll take his spot."

Andre threw for a full fifteen minutes before House returned, then spent the rest of the day shagging flies and sitting out drills along with Mack. He smiled his way through it all, as he and Mack had agreed to do. He even smiled his way through dinner, although Deets was staring daggers at him the whole time.

The next morning, when he and Mack arrived at the cage to sneak in their morning workout, Andre heard the door open behind them as soon as they'd entered.

"House, can we just—" he said. But when he turned, he didn't find House. He found Benny. Mack's roommate was timidly holding a bat with his glove threaded over the handle.

"Cool if I hit with you guys?" he asked.

"Absolutely," Andre said. "You can hit *first*." He wrapped an arm around Benny's shoulder and led him inside. "Something I've been meaning to ask you: What's your last name? I never caught it."

"I never did, either," said Mack, blushing as he followed along.

Benny grinned. "It's Mendoza," he said.

Andre's and Mack's eyes widened in unison. "Any relation to Mario?" Andre asked.

"I *wish*," the catcher replied.

On day three of the new experiment, Benny brought Reo with him.

"I figure if you guys could help Benny," Reo said, "the least I could do was get out of bed to help you."

Mack smiled. "You're too kind."

"So what now, Coach?" Benny asked Andre.

Andre looked at Mack, who nodded back at him, prodding him forward.

"Let's get it," said Andre.

CHAPTER
12

"YOU CALL THAT CONTROL?"

Miles read Mack's email—subject line "So far, so good"—five times. His chest swelled more with each pass, until he felt like a superhero in a golden-age comic book.

He stashed Wi-Fi's tablet and left the cabin for breakfast, but the details of Mack's note danced through his head as he walked from senior camp to the mess hall. At best, he figured, his idea would get his friends out of Killington. At worst, it had made their lives there better.

And in the meantime, his own life was returning to normal. That morning, he planned to go to an intermediate rocketry class. That afternoon? Perhaps another one. He hadn't got that far in planning for himself yet. He might even try to fit in a swim.

But no sooner had he left the mess hall after breakfast than he heard his name shouted from behind him.

"Miles!"

He turned to find Cassie, Nicole, and Makayla running toward him. "What's up?" he asked.

"No," Cassie said, half out of breath. "*You* what's up. What's up with *you*?"

"Yeah." Nicole studied his face. "I haven't seen anyone smile that much since Pat convinced the mess-hall cooks to make silver-dollar pancakes."

"And they're really just small pancakes!" Cassie interjected.

Miles furrowed his brow and failed to twist his mouth into a frown. "Me?" he asked. "Smiling?"

Nicole snorted. "Okay," she said. "Out with it."

Miles checked his watch. Maybe he had time for the short version.

He sat cross-legged on the junior-camp field grass and took a deep breath, then recounted everything from the beginning: how Deets had sidelined Andre and isolated Mack, then made them mow a croquet pitch in the middle of the night; how he'd come up with his plan to outsmart Deets by watching Garth; and how Mack and Andre had launched themselves into it.

"And now they're doing great. Mack's roommates are on their side, and more kids are sure to follow—which means Deets is losing his hold on the camp," he said. "And, well, it's all because of … me."

Miles gasped for air. But when he looked back up at his

friends, he didn't get the response he'd been expecting. Instead of toothy grins or high fives or applause, Nicole and Cassie gave him thousand-yard stares.

"That's …" Cassie began.

"… it!" Nicole finished.

Passing by on their way to the waterfront, Spike and Mike grunted.

"That's …" Mike started.

"… our thing!" Spike finished.

Miles did a quadruple take, then returned his attention to Cassie and Nicole. "*What's* it?" he asked.

"Yeah, what?" Makayla echoed, seeming just as concerned.

"I'm going to win so much that Garth begs for mercy," Cassie said. Then she took off running. "Thanks, Miles!"

"No, wait—!" Miles shouted, but Cassie was already halfway across the field. He watched her go, feeling his euphoria—not to mention his morning rocketry class—slipping away. "What about you?" he asked, turning to Nicole.

She raised an eyebrow. "I'd forgotten they play croquet there."

Miles had a sudden flashback to the steam table line on pizza night—and a word misheard over the noise of the kitchen.

"*Mallets*," he said flatly. "Of course."

On his way to rocketry, Miles found himself making a detour. And as he traced Cassie's steps to the ball-hockey court, he realized another reason he loved his chosen hobby.

Although it might not have seemed like it judging by his first launch of the summer, a rocket was a predictable thing. If you did everything by the book—used proper materials, followed the blueprints, accounted for weather, and so on—you got expected results.

But life wasn't like that. Too many variables.

And if the simple act of telling his story to a few friends had created two cascading chains of events, what unintended consequences would Mack and Andre's campaign have?

Miles arrived at the court and took up his post at the center line. He spotted Cassie running onto the court, her eyes burning behind her helmet's face cage. She made a beeline for Garth, who was stickhandling a ball in one of the face-off circles.

"Oh no," Miles muttered.

Cassie ran up behind him and popped the ball away.

"Hey!" Garth yelled.

"You call that control?" Cassie shouted back.

"Give it back," he growled.

Miles watched as Cassie darted into a group of Hortonia players, some of whom were stretching, some stickhandling, and some—like Alexei—just standing around, their backs to him. As Garth closed the gap on Cassie, she faked going to Alexei's right, then pulled the ball back and darted left.

But Garth was moving too fast to nail the same maneuver. Instead, he barreled right into Alexei's back, sending them both toppling to the ground as Cassie sprinted away, grinning, the ball still on her stick.

Garth groaned as he helped Alexei up. But by the time he'd grabbed his stick and re-emerged in front of the net to give chase, Cassie was already back in his end of the court. She lined up a slap shot directly at him from the blue line, but at the last minute, she redirected the ball to the side so it flew into the top corner of the net.

"All yours, Garth," she said.

Garth scowled, too angry even to remind her of his preferred name. "Keep it up, Ramos," he said.

"Oh, I will," she chirped, running to the other end to find another ball.

Pat walked over to Miles. "Looks like someone wants a visit from the poison-ivy fairy," he said, a grateful tone in his voice.

Miles had the distinct feeling that he hadn't relayed the right parts of his plan, or that Cassie had misunderstood them. She wasn't being more herself. She was being Garth.

Next time go with the long version, he thought to himself.

CHAPTER 13

"YOU HAVE VISITORS"

"What stinks?"

Mack woke up sniffing at the air of his dorm room. Again he'd had a nightmare, this time about the camp turning to cardboard and falling away beneath his and Andre's feet. He found his bed solid and squarely underneath him, but the stench—that wasn't a dream.

"Hey, guys, what's that—?" He tried to scratch his scalp but didn't feel hair. Instead, he found something soft, padded … cotton.

Socks.

Dirty socks.

On his head.

It was the old Camp Average prank. And it had been played on *him*.

Mack would've been touched—if he weren't so grossed out.

"Ew!" he yelled and rolled out of his bed to the floor, all four socks falling off his head at once.

Benny and Reo burst out laughing as Mack bolted for the bathroom.

"I take back what I said!" Benny yelled. "That *is* funny!"

After lathering his head in hand soap and rinsing with cold water, Mack returned to his room and swore revenge on his roommates. Then he got dressed and headed out the door with them. It was 5:00 a.m. They had been getting up early for pre-practice practice for a week now.

It had solidified their friendship and helped their games—Andre had dominated in a second intra-camp clash—but Mack had lost hope that Miles's plan would get them kicked out. Deets was stomping around camp so much he might as well have been a *T. rex*, and the boys had joked that they should keep a glass of water handy to know when he was coming. All they'd have to do was watch for the ripples.

But he hadn't *done* anything. Hadn't even *said* anything.

If the dominoes were going to fall the way Miles said they would, wouldn't they have fallen already?

As he reached the batting cage for yet another session of hitting and feeding balls into the machine, Mack realized that this plan was no longer a means to an end. This was closer to an end in itself.

And yet he didn't really believe that, either. There was something else.

As much as all-day baseball practice wasn't his first choice of summer activity—or second or fifth or fifteenth (those would all have involved at least some kind of water sport)—Mack had to admit that it was pretty cushy by most standards.

Too cushy, really.

He looked around the cavernous space and found Andre at the far end, tightening the Velcro on his glove. In Mack's mind, the two of them were Second World War soldiers having tea in the middle of the wrong army's base camp. But for some unknown reason, the opposing general refused to toss them into the brig—instead, he just glared at them and stomped around.

This *wasn't* the end for them and their war with Deets, and Mack knew it. He just didn't know what was coming next. Or when it would arrive.

"Hey, Mack!" Andre shouted, snapping him out of his reverie. "You're up!"

∾

Later that morning on the practice field, House had the boys stand facing each other about ten feet apart, then drop into proper fielding position with their knees bent and butts low to the ground. From there, they rolled the ball to their partners, who fielded it with their gloves and transferred it to their throwing hands to roll back.

"Okay, now pick up the pace as you go!" House told them. "See if you can knock out your partner by—"

Tinny punk music filled the air. The coach pulled out his smartphone and walked away without another look.

"Hello?" he asked, his voice trailing off.

While the drill continued around him, Mack watched the coach carefully. He had seen House take phone calls during practice several times. But this time, he wasn't ducking behind the shed. His body language was casual, giving nothing away. Yet Mack didn't feel that it was hiding anything, either.

This wasn't Deets. This was something else.

House finished the call and jogged back to them. "Mack, Andre—let's go."

"What's up?"

House shrugged. "You have visitors."

CHAPTER
14

"STICK AROUND FOR
THE COMEBACK?"

In most ways, Killington and Camp Average couldn't have been more different. But both camps were united on a pretty simple "no visitors" policy. Even parents could visit only once a summer, and that day was still weeks away.

Even stranger, Mack and Andre had been asked—in front of several campmates—to report to the country club side of camp.

"Nobody gets to go to the country club side!" Benny had whispered excitedly.

"What did you guys do?" Reo asked. "And was it good or bad?"

Andre thought for a second. "Always tough to tell."

He and Mack ditched their gear in Andre's dorm, then skirted around the clubhouse and crossed over the hedge-lined ridge that separated the two worlds.

The country club half of camp was even more brilliant in the daylight. The quaint streetlamps they'd noticed before faded into the background as rose gardens, water fountains, and hedges cut to look like wild animals took center stage.

"Is that a puma?" Mack asked, staring at one hedge with large jaws, short pointy ears, and a long tail.

"I think it's a bobcat," Andre said.

"What's the difference?"

Andre stopped in his tracks. Then both boys said at the same time: "Miles would know."

House had told them their destination would be obvious when they saw it, so they simply continued on into foreign territory and soon found themselves passing the tennis courts.

"Think this has anything to do with the other night?" Andre asked.

As they came in sight of the croquet pitch, Mack nodded somberly. "Wouldn't doubt it."

The area was abuzz with activity. A mix of adult officials and kids in eerily bright, clean clothes—Andre guessed they were country club campers—stood at the edges of the pitch, looking inwards.

Andre looked down at his and Mack's dirty rumpled T-shirts and sweatpants and felt massively underdressed.

But that was only one of his concerns.

"What if something got messed up with the pitch? Like the grass is too short and now they can't play?" he asked breathlessly as they walked ever nearer. "Or if some stuff went missing? My fingerprints are all over that mower! This could all be part of a shakedown. They want us to return to the scene of the crime!"

"I don't know," Mack said. "Would someone refer to police detectives as visitors?"

"House might!" Andre answered.

As it turned out, they had not been called to trim the croquet pitch or answer for the manner in which it had been trimmed. They were there to see …

"Nicole?!" Mack pointed at the pitch.

Andre followed Mack's gaze through a group of kids and saw—in a white polo shirt, white shorts, and white shoes—a girl whom Mack had known since they were six years old.

"What's *she* doing here?!" he asked.

"Playing croquet," Andre deadpanned.

"I get that," Mack said. "But, like, is she here for us, or … ?"

"Classic Mack," interrupted a voice behind them. "Always thinking everything's about you."

Mack blushed as he and Andre turned to find Nicole's best friend Makayla. She was standing behind them in an outfit identical to Nicole's, a mocking look on her face and her hands on her hips.

"Hey!" Andre shouted, giving her a hug. "Croquet, huh?"

"Yeah, Nicole decided to play as soon as we heard the Swish City tournament was canceled," Makayla said. "She convinced me to join in by saying this would be basically like golf." Makayla's mom was a professional golfer, and her daughter had inherited her natural ability on the links.

"And is it?" Andre asked.

Makayla snorted out a little laugh. "Not even close."

"But," Mack said, still confused, "how did you get here?"

"We asked," said Makayla. "Nicole remembered that Killington holds croquet tournaments all the time, and Cheryl entered us in this one. She still felt bad about Swish City getting canceled, so she wanted to help."

"Well then, how did you get *us* here?"

Makayla rolled her eyes. "We *asked*," she said again. "Not everything has to be difficult, you know."

The newly formed trio watched as Nicole stood before a red ball on the far side of the pitch, lining up a shot. Despite himself, Andre looked at the immaculately trimmed grass with no small degree of pride. But he also noticed that it had changed slightly from the other night. Now it boasted six things that looked like large white staples sticking up out of the ground.

Nicole swung the mallet between her legs and hammered the ball, which sailed a few inches wide of its intended target.

"How do you know which wicket to go through first?" Mack asked Makayla as Nicole swung her fist in anger.

Makayla shot him a condescending smile. "First, they're called hoops—not wickets," she said.

"Right," Mack said. "Because they're so round and everything."

"I don't make up the names," she said. "And second, you go up one side of the pitch, then down the far one, and then back up the middle." She pulled a notebook and pencil from her bag and sketched a kind of map.

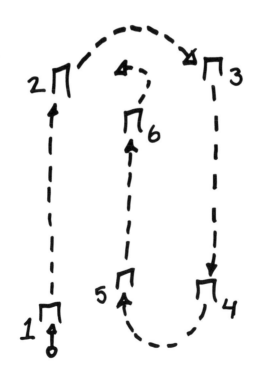

"See?" she asked.

Mack couldn't see much of anything. "Clear as a bell," he said sarcastically.

On the pitch, Nicole seemed to be muttering to herself. Then she noticed the boys for the first time, and her eyes lit up.

"Time-out!" she shouted in the middle of her opponent's swing, causing the girl to lose control of her mallet entirely. It sailed over an official's head and into the woods.

Nicole dropped her own mallet, then charged off the pitch at top speed. She didn't slow down at all as she grabbed both boys around their necks in a suffocating bear hug.

"Nice ... to see ... you ... too," Mack wheezed.

Nicole loosened her grip. "You made it. I didn't know if you would."

"Neither did we," Andre said, rubbing his neck. "We just got called over here a few minutes ago."

"So how's the tournament going?" Mack asked.

"Horribly! We seemed to be getting better in practice," she said, "but these guys are on another level. Makayla lost 14–0, and I'm on my way to the same. Not like we care that much."

"So you *are* here to see us!" Mack crowed. "I knew it!"

Nicole and Makayla shared a glance.

"Classic Mack," Nicole said, unknowingly repeating her friend. "We for sure suck at this, and I kind of hate sucking at things. But sometimes it's just about the competition, you know? Competing and sucking is better than not competing at all."

Mack shrugged his shoulders. "Maybe," he said. "But it's still not better than just going to the waterfront."

"Classic Mack!" said Andre, Nicole, and Makayla in unison.

Mack took a deep breath, smiling sheepishly.

Andre watched his friend squirm with no small amount of delight. "It's okay, man, we'll—"

"Excuse me, miss?" a Killington official broke in, catching Nicole's attention. "We have located your opponent's mallet, and the game can resume."

"Stick around for the comeback?" she asked, turning to Mack and Andre.

Andre flopped to the ground and crossed his legs, pulling Mack down with him.

"Obviously," he said.

CHAPTER
15

"YOU'RE KICKING ME OUT?"

For the rest of the day, Mack took questions from every kid he came in contact with.

"What was it like?"

"How many water fountains were there?"

"Did you find the smoothie pool?!"

He ran through the answers over and over again, right up until he crawled into bed and closed his eyes, falling asleep almost instantly.

He woke up when he heard a knock on the door. He didn't know how long he'd been out, but he heard his roommates groan instinctively.

Must be not quite morning, he thought.

"Somebody else want to get this one?" he mumbled, but his two roommates offered only silence in return. No one ever came to bother *them* before sunrise.

"I'll take that as a no."

Mack rolled out of bed and shuffled to the door,

convinced he knew who was waiting on the other side.

"House, what is it—" he began as he pulled open the door.

But instead of his coach, he found a smiling woman in a navy-blue skirt and matching suit jacket with her dark hair in a tight bun.

"Hello, Mr. Jones," she said. "My name is Calista. I'm the head housing administrator here at Camp Killington. I'm afraid I have some not great news for you."

Mack stared back at her, partly out of grogginess and partly because he was studying her face, which had a slightly embarrassed look on it. The overworked gears of his brain whirred to life. Embarrassed. At his door. This early in the morning. Why?

"Mr. Jones?"

"What's happening?" Mack asked, unmoving.

Calista's cheeks reddened. She smoothed her skirt. "There's been an … administrative error. I'm afraid we don't have room for you at camp after all."

Mack looked back at his lower bunk, which he confirmed was empty and still fit one person. He returned his gaze to Calista.

"Hmm?" he said.

"We have arranged for you to spend the rest of the summer at Camp Aver—er, Camp Avalon."

Mack blinked. "You're kicking me out?"

"Oh no! No, no," Calista said, holding her hands up and waving them frantically. "We would never!"

Mack smacked Calista's hands like she was going for a high ten. "You're kicking me out!" He pumped his fist. "Miles really *is* a genius!"

Calista's look of panic morphed into one of confusion. "Huh?" she asked.

"Nothing. How long do I have?"

"I'm afraid time is of the essence," Calista said, checking her watch.

"All I need is two minutes."

Mack ducked back into his room without closing the door, a kind of chant running over and over in his head: *We did it. We're getting out.*

He took two leaping steps to the bed to pack. Only ... there was nothing to pack. His duffel bag still doubled as a dresser, so all he had to do was stuff his sleeping bag inside and change into some traveling clothes.

Two minutes? he thought. *Make that thirty seconds.*

Mack threw on shorts and a T-shirt, and slid on his flip-flops. Then he shouldered his bag and strode toward the door.

"Mack?" Benny asked in a raspy voice from the top bunk. "What's going on?"

Mack felt a pang of remorse. He was so excited to

get back to his old friends, he hadn't even thought to say goodbye to his new ones. He turned to find Benny propping himself up on an elbow and rubbing the sleep from his eyes. The boy squinted at him in the darkness, then—in an instant—his eyes became as large and round as life preservers.

"You're leaving?!" he shouted.

Mack shushed him. "No!" he said. "I mean … yes. I mean … they say I *have* to leave."

Benny frowned. "You don't seem surprised. Were you expecting this?"

Mack briefly considered lying. Then he thought better of it. Sharing a bunk bed with someone, he knew from experience, was as good as having a permanent lie detector.

"Kind of."

"And you didn't tell us?"

"No."

"And you weren't even going to say goodbye?"

Mack looked at the ground.

"Then fine." Benny turned to the wall and pulled his covers halfway up his head. "I've got nothing to say to you, either."

"Hey, Benny," Mack said, dropping his duffel on the ground. "Come on, man. I'm sorry. It was a mistake."

But Benny didn't move.

"Mr. Jones?" Calista asked from the doorway.

"Just one more minute," Mack pleaded.

He tried to rouse Benny a dozen more times before finally giving up. He turned in defeat to Reo, who was now sitting up with his tablet in his lap.

"Smooth move," he said as he watched himself hit a line drive in real time, then watched it again backward in slow motion.

"Thanks," Mack said icily. "See you around."

"Not likely," said Reo absently.

Mack snorted. He was pretty sure Reo meant it in a mean way, but he couldn't help thinking Pat would've appreciated the delivery.

He shouldered his duffel bag again, took one last look around the tiny room that had been his home for two weeks, and walked out the door, pulling it closed behind him.

"Where to?" he asked.

Calista smiled. "Right this way."

She led him down the hall and through the Mendoza building foyer. Mack got a weird sense of his life moving in reverse as they retraced the steps he'd taken on the first night of camp. They passed the Ruth building and about ten gazebos, and finally arrived in front of the camp office.

Calista pulled the duffel off Mack's shoulders, placed it in the back of a white van, and opened the door for him. He happily hopped inside and found … no one.

The door slammed shut behind him.

"Wait!" Mack yelled, fumbling with the buttons on the door's armrest, trying to roll the window down. Instead, he turned on both the air-conditioning and the seat warmer, giving his face a blast of cold and his butt a blast of heat.

"Where's Andre?" he yelled to Calista through the closed window.

The blue-capped driver furrowed his brow as they pulled away from the curb. He met Mack's eyes in the rearview mirror.

"Andre who?" he asked.

CHAPTER 16

"DID YOU *SEW* THIS?"

Basking in a pool of morning sunlight, a book called *Houston, We Have a Hobby* in his lap, Miles tried to focus on the words on the page. But he couldn't. Not with all the shouting going on.

"Did you *sew* this?" Pat screamed. "I woke up with it on my bed!"

Pat was looming over Garth's bunk, holding up what appeared to be a green blanket. But it was made up of dozens of small leaves, each shaped like a cartoon flame, strung one after another. Miles noticed that his friend was holding the blanket by the corners with half a roll's worth of toilet paper wrapped around each hand.

Garth tried to put on an innocent face, but it quickly gave way to a proud grin. "I had to work a needle and thread wearing cleaning gloves!" he gushed. "It took me three nights! You like it?"

Miles sighed heavily. It was bad enough he had to worry about Cassie's ongoing feud with Garth—he had tried for days to get her to ease up on the newcomer, but each time he broached the subject, she seemed to think he was joking. Otherwise, she said, why would he have given her the idea in the first place?

But now, in what should have been his quiet moments, he also had to listen to Pat and Garth go at it in the cabin.

"Well, it's obviously exquisite," Pat admitted, laying the blanket delicately on the floor. "But it's also my nightmare! Stop it with the pranks already."

From the back of the room, Wi-Fi and Nelson quietly chittered. "That's hilarious," Nelson said, staring at the tablet like he was narrating something. "Pat telling *someone else* to cut out the pranks."

Miles was about to ask again what they were up to, but Pat quickly regained his attention.

"When I gave you poison ivy—"

"So you admit it!" Garth cut him off.

"It was an *accident*! I didn't *mean* for it to happen," Pat asserted forcefully. "I just hoped you'd waste your hiking time looking for a peak that doesn't exist. But I swear to you, I wouldn't do something like that on purpose."

Garth scowled as he took this in. Then he seemed to take a breath, and the tension eased out of his face and shoulders. Miles began to hope that this agonizing back-and-forth was finally coming to an end.

Then Pat opened his mouth again.

"That said …" he began.

Miles watched Garth's shoulders tense up again. His face jumped to full scowl mode.

"That said *what*?" he asked.

"It was also karma," Pat said. "You guys deserved it for the way you treated Mack at that social—and, you know, for not looking where you were going on the hike."

The room went dead silent.

"And when it really comes down to it," Pat continued, "I basically regret nothing."

Miles heard Nelson and Wi-Fi gasp. Sitting on their adjacent beds, Spike and Mike dropped their jaws in unison. Alexei … didn't seem to be paying attention. He was looking at his fingernails.

Meanwhile, Garth's face was a kaleidoscope of emotions as Pat's words twisted their way into his brain.

"Well, then," he said after a while, "I guess I don't, either."

"But I do!" Laker broke in, washing his hands at the back of the room with the sound of the toilet flushing behind him.

He got between the two combatants and, with a look, forced them each to take a step back.

"I regret giving up my own cabin, and I definitely regret agreeing to live in *this one*," Laker sputtered. "No more poison ivy in here or anywhere." His gaze darted from Garth to Pat to the poison ivy quilt on the floor. "*I may be stuck here for the summer, but you aren't.* The next one of you who even says the words 'poison ivy' is moving into the lodge."

"But, Laker, the lodge is for—" Pat protested.

"No buts!" Laker pointed at the homemade blanket on the floor. "Clean this up—*carefully*—or I'll send both of you to the lodge right now."

Garth looked expectantly at Pat, who snorted derisively. "Oh, *allow me*," he said, holding up his toilet-paper-mummified hands.

Pat delicately balled up the blanket and carried it to the garbage can at the back of the room, Miles hot on his heels.

"So long, old friend!" Garth called to his creation.

Once Pat had finished stuffing both the quilt and his TP gloves into the can, Miles grabbed him by the shoulders and shook.

"Pat!" he whisper-shrieked into his face. "Garth was going to accept your explanation! We were so close to getting a cabin where we could hear ourselves think! You were out!"

"Maybe I don't want out," Pat said. "If it's a war this guy wants and he won't listen to reason, then maybe I'm in."

"Yeah, but … what do you mean?" Miles asked nervously. "What are you going to do?"

Pat tilted his head to one side, looking at the ceiling. Then he squinted one eye. And raised his fist under his chin.

"Pat?" Miles asked after a while.

"Oh," Pat said, "I got nothing. I was just seeing how long I could get you to watch me 'think.' It was like thirty seconds."

Miles ran his hands through his hair, pulling the skin on his forehead and exposing the whites of his eyes behind his glasses.

"Whatever," he said angrily. "You do what you want. I can't handle this anymore."

Miles checked his watch and discovered it was time for breakfast. Maybe he could drown his sorrows in pancake syrup.

He walked the length of the cabin and yanked open the door in a rage—only to find a tall boy with unkempt brown hair standing on the porch, a duffel bag slung over his shoulder.

"Mack," Miles breathed.

"MACK?!" yelled several different people from inside the cabin.

With dumbstruck looks on their faces, Pat, Nelson, Wi-Fi, Spike, and Mike awkwardly crowded the doorway. Then they crashed through it to mob their friend.

Mack had returned from Killington.

"Room for one more?" he asked, a half smile quickly appearing on and then disappearing from his face as his roommates bear-hugged him off the ground.

Miles nearly burst out laughing. His plan had worked! Why had he been so worried? His plans were *great*, and Mack's reappearance proved it!

Then he realized two things at once, and the laugh never made it past the base of his throat.

Cabin 23 didn't actually have room for one more.

And Mack was alone.

CHAPTER
17

"NOW IS NOT THE TIME!"

At the first sight of Oak Lake, the glistening body of water upon which Camp Average sat, Mack knew he was home. But instead of making a beeline for the beach—his undisputed happy place—he bolted in the opposite direction.

So many thoughts competed for space in his head. He and his best friend had gone toe to toe with a bully bent on ruining their summer. Had they won? Kind of. Lost? Almost definitely.

Suddenly the two words—"winning" and "losing"— seemed insufficient, like there should be another one between them. And so Mack quickened his steps toward the one person he knew who might have it.

Now, standing on the porch of what should have been his cabin, Mack watched the faces of his friends droop until they looked like he felt—confused and maybe a little hurt. Who could tell?

"I got kicked out," he said finally. "Andre didn't." Then

he thought about it for a second. "At least ... I don't think he did. They didn't really give me a rundown."

"But how?" Nelson asked. "Why?"

Mack locked eyes with Miles, who turned beet red. "Long story," he replied.

His friends continued staring at him, but Mack didn't know what to do next. Bump some fists? Tell the long story? Unpack his bag? He could tell no one else knew what to do, either.

None of his friends, anyway.

"Kicked out of a summer camp?!" called out a boy at the back of the group. "Hilarious."

"Garth!" Pat shouted in reply.

"Forehead!"

"Now is not the time!"

Garth, Mack thought. *Right.*

In his current state of bewilderment, he had forgotten about the boy's existence, let alone the fact that he was occupying what should have been Mack's bed. He realized that unpacking his bag wasn't even an option—he had nothing to unpack it into.

"Hey," Garth said, turning on Pat, "Wayne Gretzky says, 'There's no time like the present.'"

Miles rolled his eyes. "I'm pretty sure he didn't. That quote is, like, five hundred years old."

"Gordie Howe, then," said Garth, smiling.

Mack watched Miles smack his forehead. Then he felt a kind of rumbling. It seemed far off at first, but very quickly drew closer.

"Is that … an earthquake?" asked Wi-Fi.

"It's an earthquake!" confirmed Pat hastily.

Panic spread immediately. "Everybody!" Laker leapt to his feet. "Get to a doorway!"

"We're already in the doorway!" Pat yelled back as the group formed a tighter and tighter scrum in the structural integrity of the doorframe.

"Who's stepping on my ankle?" Nelson asked.

"That's *my* ankle!" Pat shouted.

Mack followed his friends' lead, spinning in place so he could plant his feet and press his back into the group.

"Guys?" he said, looking out into the common area in front of the cabin. "You might want to see this."

The boys craned their necks to find what must have been a hundred kids running at them, with Cassie at the front of the group. She bounded onto the porch and hug-tackled Mack, her shoulder connecting—hard—with his stomach.

"Oof," he grunted.

"Right back at you, big guy," she said, panting.

As the stampede formed a giant semicircle around cabin 23, the kids in the doorway peeled themselves apart.

"Some earthquake, Pat." Nelson rubbed his ankle. "I think it was a twenty-five on the Richter scale."

"Why blame me?!" Pat fired back. "Wi-Fi started it."

"I just asked the question!" Wi-Fi protested.

Cassie doubled over from exertion. "I was in line for pancakes!" she told Mack breathlessly. "Some guy said he thought he saw you getting out of a van. Obviously, I had to find out right away. When I ran out of the mess hall"—she glanced at the crowd behind her—"I guess everyone else followed."

She wiped her brow with the back of one hand, then raised a pancake to her mouth with the other.

Nelson grunted in disgust.

"What?" she asked her brother. "I was supposed to let it go to *waste*?"

As Cassie finished chewing, Mack felt a hundred pairs of eyes on him, waiting for … well, he didn't know what exactly. He felt he was in a play where everyone had forgotten the words.

Luckily, Cassie always had a few in the tank. She wiped her mouth, then turned her attention to the kids gathered on the porch. She dove in headfirst, elbowing stomachs and pulling shoulders, then dug her way back out.

"Where's Andre?" she asked Mack, frowning.

Mack threw his head back in frustration. "Andre didn't

get out," he shouted loudly enough for all to hear. "Andre is *not here*."

"And that is *not bad*!" Garth cackled from inside the cabin.

Mack opened his mouth, but Cassie got there first.

"Okay," she said. "That's it."

She parted the group of boys in the doorway until she stood face-to-face with Garth, who had a smug look and his arms crossed.

"Get out," she said. "You're mean. You don't get to live here anymore."

Garth stood stock-still for a moment, unsure of whether she had that kind of power. He shoved his hands into the pockets of his shorts.

"No," he said in a voice lacking confidence.

"Yes," Cassie replied. "Your bed belongs to Mack."

"*No*," he said more strongly. "I won my place in this cabin fair and square. Mack didn't even want to go here this summer."

"Neither did you. *You're* here because Mother Nature tried to kill your camp. Which is starting to seem like something she did on purpose."

"Doesn't change things."

Cassie popped the last morsel of pancake into her mouth and chewed slowly without breaking eye contact with Garth. Finally she swallowed.

"One game," she said.

"Huh?" he grunted.

"One ball-hockey game," she said. "Camp Average versus Camp Hortonia. One week from today. If we win, you give Mack's bed back. And you lay off. No more bullying."

Mack felt like he'd been fired from the play. Now he was a spectator, but he'd missed at least the first act. What did Cassie have against Garth?

Meanwhile, Pat's face lit up. He whispered in Cassie's ear.

"And you have to be Pat's best friend," she told Garth. "You'll admit you were wrong about him the whole time and apologize for everything."

Garth raised an eyebrow. "What if we win?"

"You won't."

"But if we do."

"Not gonna happen."

"Humor me!"

"If you win," Cassie said, "Hortonia gets this whole cabin. We move out, and you can move in whoever you want."

"Yeah!" Pat shouted, sticking a finger in Garth's face. Then he furrowed his brow.

"Wait …" said Mike.

"… WHAT?" shouted Spike.

"Cassie," Miles implored, "you don't even sleep in this—!"

"It's a bet!" shouted Garth before any further protests could be made. "No adults involved. No way they'd sign off."

Cassie nodded. Then she saw Laker at the back of the room.

"Don't look at me," he said, lying back on his bed. "The only thing I care about is poison ivy."

Cassie and Garth shook hands. The deal was done.

As the members of cabin 23 set in on Cassie, Mack tried to push through the crowd to dump his bag in the lounge Miles had told him about. But he made it only a single step before Nicole and Makayla showed up, bursting into the space between the porch and the crowd.

"Mack?!" they shouted in unison.

Mack let his bag fall off his shoulder. It dropped to the porch with a thud. "In the flesh," he mumbled weakly.

He spun away from the door to find both girls looking nothing like they had for the croquet tournament at Killington. Instead of their country club whites, each one was dressed in Camp Average gear—and covered head to toe in brambles and soot.

"Where were *you*?" he asked.

Nicole smoothed her hair, pulling out a strand of

spiderweb in the process. "Overnight camping trip," she said.

Then she frowned and scanned the porch. Mack knew what was coming.

"Where's Andre?" she asked.

CHAPTER
18

"SO ... WHAT NOW?"

While it was never Mack's idea of fun to wake up before dawn for hitting practice, it also wasn't like him to be late to the cage. So when Andre arrived that morning and found himself alone, he immediately began imagining worst-case scenarios.

Scenarios involving Mack accidentally stepping on Reo's tablet and being chased all over camp.

Scenarios involving endless bathroom trips—Mack's personal menu *did* seem heavy on the chili, now that Andre thought about it.

Scenarios involving House asking him to touch up the croquet pitch on his own.

But he and Mack had been on their best behavior for days. And if they were going to be punished for trying hard and making friends with Deets's fans, wouldn't that punishment have already kicked into gear?

Maybe Mack was just hungry, Andre mused. He left

the cage and walked to the clubhouse, but the chefs said they hadn't seen Mack yet.

Andre carried on to the Mendoza building, but he found no one there, either (not even in the bathroom).

Shrugging, he walked back to the cages and discovered actual living, breathing kids huddled on a bench at the far end of the cavernous space.

Finally, he thought.

As he approached, though, he didn't get a sense of things returning to normal. Just the opposite. Benny and Reo were there, but Mack wasn't with them.

"What's going on?" Andre asked when they turned to him with wounded looks.

After a long moment, Benny spoke up. "A camp administrator came to our door this morning," he explained. "She said there was no room for Mack here anymore. It didn't make sense. But … he said he'd been expecting it."

Andre's eyes bugged out. No one had come to *his* room. "What?!" he shouted. "Where is he now?"

"Gone," Benny mumbled, kicking the leg of the bench with the heel of his sneaker.

"But," Andre began, "why would—?"

"Long story short?" Reo crossed his arms. "He bailed."

Andre's eyes returned to their normal size. His chest

puffed out involuntarily, and his hands balled into fists by his sides.

"I'm going to say this once," he replied quietly. "Mack Jones never bailed on anybody in his life."

Benny and Reo stopped moving. For a second, they seemed to stop breathing.

"Do you even know why Mack came here this summer?" Andre continued. "He wasn't trying to prove anything or take anyone's spot. He did it so I wouldn't be alone."

Andre told the boys about the deal he'd made with Deets the summer before, and about how Mack had spent the entire spring trying out so he could be there on the first day of camp.

"He knew I wasn't going to be … welcomed," Andre said, looking from one boy to the other as they avoided his gaze, "so he gave up his entire summer to help *me*." Andre threw up his hands. "I mean, this side of camp doesn't even *have* a pool."

The idea hung in the air as the three stared at the brushed concrete floor. Then Reo stood to look Andre in the eye.

"Sorry," he said. "I was just mad." He took a breath. "Guess I didn't plan on making friends this summer. And I really wasn't prepared for one of them leaving."

Andre grinned a sad grin. "Yeah, well, Mack can have that effect on people."

Benny squirmed a little on the bench. "So … what now?"

"You guys want to quit?" Andre asked. The question drew two blank looks. "Me, neither. This is a baseball camp. Let's play baseball."

"But …" Reo began.

Andre raised an eyebrow. "But what?"

"We've got three people. That's one pitcher, one hitter, and one guy standing around. Not exactly efficient."

"Maybe," Benny said warily, "we could invite a few more people to the morning sessions?"

"Better you than me," Andre said. "But suit yourselves."

As Benny and Reo made their way to the nearest cage to fire up the pitching machine, Andre flopped down on a bench to tighten his cleats. He thought back to his first meeting with Mack at Camp Average when they were seven.

He remembered a tall, fearless-looking kid basically dragging a tiny homesick boy in glasses from place to place at orientation. Whenever adults approached to ask Miles how he was doing, Mack would step in. "He's fine!" he'd say. "Can you point us to the rocketry … place?"

As if he already had the run of the camp. Or was allowed out of the sight of a counselor.

Andre also remembered discovering that the two boys were in his cabin, then bringing his own friend from back home to Miles's bunk.

"I'm Andre," he remembered saying, "and this is Willy. His friends call him Wi-Fi."

"Why?" Miles had asked, wiping away tears.

"Wi-Fi not?" chimed in a skinny boy they'd eventually know as Pat.

In Andre's mind's eye, he could see seven-year-old Mack shooting him a grateful look.

"Mack," he'd said like a grown-up, holding out his hand.

Back in the real world, thirteen-year-old Andre finished tying his shoes just as House walked into the building.

"Slow start today," he said, glancing at the empty cages. "And you're down a batter. What gives?"

Andre glared at the man who'd been put in charge of both their whereabouts and their torment. As if he didn't know "what gave."

"They kicked Mack out," he said in a strangled voice.

House frowned. "No, they didn't."

Benny took a step toward his dorm supervisor. "Yeah, they did."

"We saw them do it," Reo added.

"No," he said, more to himself than the boys in front of him. "They wouldn't."

Andre cast him an appraising glance. "You mean, you really didn't know?"

House shook his head.

"And you weren't on board with this?"

"Of course not!" House said loudly, his face turning red.

He turned abruptly away from the group and walked halfway down the row of batting cages, only to wheel and turn back. He did three of these circuits, muttering the whole time.

"'Just go along with it,' he said. 'You'll get fired if you don't,' he said."

"Uh … House?" Andre asked. "What are you talking about?"

"Nothing," the coach grunted. Then he made a beeline for the door. "Let's go. Time for breakfast."

CHAPTER
19

"PREPARE FOR IMPACT!"

Maybe everyone had just forgotten what time ball-hockey tryouts started.

No, Cassie thought, *just about everyone in camp was in the mess hall when I stood up to announce the details.*

It was the morning after she had set the terms of the showdown. And since she had issued the challenge on her own, she had let her fellow campers decide whether to join in the fight. Of course, she'd assumed everyone would be in. And yet somehow, when she looked around the ball-hockey court, she found only Pat, Spike, and Mike. Nelson and Wi-Fi were sitting in the last row of the stands, but they showed no signs of actually wanting to play.

Laker, who'd agreed to coach only if Cassie agreed to stop coming into their cabin in the middle of the day, was leaning all the way back on the bleachers. He had a red ball cap pulled low over his eyes.

So as it stood, they didn't have enough players for a full

line of three forwards, two defenders, and a goalie, and their coach appeared to be asleep. She wasn't even sure he knew how to play the game.

"Let's give them five more minutes," she said to the waiting trio of players.

"You said that ..." started Mike.

"... five minutes ago," finished Spike.

Pat grinned. "Hey, look at it this way," he told the twins. "At least you know you've made the team."

"This is serious, Pat!" Cassie admonished.

"I'm being serious!"

"We're two players short of a full line!"

"That's what I'm talking about!" Pat said. "If you cut one of us, then we're suddenly *three* players short."

Cassie shook her head and spun away. Just then, she saw a head of brown hair bobbing up and down behind the boards along the edge of the court. She racked her brains but couldn't come up with a single person at camp who couldn't see over the three-foot wall that circled the playing surface.

"Hello?" she shouted.

Cassie heard someone take a deep breath. Then the brown hair shot upward, revealing a small, bespectacled boy beneath it.

"Miles?" she asked. "What's the deal?"

Miles climbed over the boards, his cheeks as red as cherries.

"I, uh …" he said, "just wanted to find out how you were doing."

Cassie gestured to the mostly empty court. "See for yourself. We're doing great," she said sarcastically.

"Yeah," Miles said, his face returning to its normal color. "I kind of figured."

"What do you mean you figured?" she asked, taking a threatening step toward him. "You *expected* no one to show up to my ball-hockey tryouts?"

Miles reddened again. "Well, yeah," he said. "After what Garth has been saying."

Cassie grabbed Miles by the front of his green button-down shirt. Two years separated the two, but the younger girl had half an inch of height on the older boy.

"What's Garth been saying?" she growled.

Pat chimed in. "Oh, yeah, I heard that, too," he said. "A bunch of stuff about how he's going to make mincemeat of any Camp Average kid who plays on the team, how he knows a kind of karate that's banned in fifty countries, yada yada yada."

Cassie let go of Miles, and the boy dropped back onto his heels.

"You knew about this?" She turned on Pat, instantly

questioning her own taste in future prom dates. "And you didn't think to pass that info along?"

Pat gave her a skeptical look. "If you want me to come tell you every time Garth does something terrible, you're not going to have time to breathe."

Cassie threw her hands in the air and walked away from the group. "Forget it."

At first, she was just storming off. But then the storming seemed to take on a life of its own. Soon, Cassie found herself marching past the blue line, behind the net, and back up the boards on the opposite side of the court. She felt the boys' eyes following her. She didn't care. She needed to think. And apparently to walk.

Cassie may not have heard what Garth had been up to, but she knew what her own campmates thought of her deal. Had she gone too far? Had she bet something that wasn't hers? Had she dragged everyone else into a crusade of her own, as Mack had been accused of doing at least twice?

No, she thought, crossing the blue line on the opposite end of the court. *This isn't about a cabin. This is about Camp Average. And that belongs to all of us.*

She and Nelson were home-schooled. They'd never belonged to a group this big. In fact, that's essentially what her brother had told her when he got home after his first summer at the camp: he had felt like he belonged.

And now she felt the same. She might not have been coming here for as long, but this was as much her home as it was anyone's.

"Cassie?" Miles called, a note of concern in his voice. "You okay?"

But she could barely hear him. As she passed behind the court's second net, she thought about the stories Nelson had told about that infamous baseball tournament. How no one had thought they could win. How Miles had learned to bunt in a few days. How Mack had picked up a clutch single when the team needed it most.

Then she conjured memories of last summer's basketball tournament, when the boys and girls had joined forces and played under the Camp Average banner—officially—for the first time ever. She had watched from the sidelines, passing out headbands, but had felt like part of the team.

Cassie walked up the boards, bearing down on Miles, Pat, Spike, and Mike. The boys parted to let her pass, but she stopped between the twins, turning the loosely arranged group into a kind of horseshoe-shaped huddle. Wi-Fi and Nelson leaned in from the bleachers, waiting for her to speak. Laker started to snore.

"I know what we've got to do," she said.

Cassie leveled her gaze at Miles. He looked back at her,

uncertainty written all over his face. Then his eyes went wide, as if he could read her thoughts.

"No," he said, shaking his head. "Uh-uh. No."

"Yes," she said. They'd tried the logical choices. Now they needed to try the illogical ones. "We need *you*."

"But," Miles said, panicked, "what about Garth?"

"What *about* him?!" Cassie shouted. "You heard Laker in the cabin yesterday."

"Hmm?" Laker said, waking suddenly upon hearing his name.

"If Garth does anything to you or anyone else, Laker's going to send him packing. He won't risk it. Not when he's this close to getting the cabin all to himself."

"That's true," Laker mused, seeming to fall immediately back to sleep.

Cassie watched Miles take in this information, his eyes darting back and forth in a whir of motion, as if he were one of those giant antique computers that took up whole rooms. Finally, his features came to a rest.

"Fine," he said, summoning all the courage he could. "I'll play."

"I knew you would," she said, "but we still need at least one more player."

Pat, Spike, and Mike looked over the boards to where Nelson and Wi-Fi were now standing, tablet in hand.

"Don't look at us," Nelson said.

"Very busy," Wi-Fi added.

Cassie twisted up a corner of her mouth. "Care to elaborate?"

Nelson locked eyes with Wi-Fi. Then both boys turned back to the group.

"No," Wi-Fi said.

"We're making a documentary," Nelson blurted.

Miles snapped his fingers. "I should've guessed that!" he grunted angrily at himself.

"What's it about?" Cassie asked.

Wi-Fi threw his hands up in the air. "It's about *life*," he said in annoyance. "About the precious moments that bind us together and make us human."

Nelson shrugged. "Or, like, just about the summer. What's been going on around camp," he said. "But we're pretty into it."

Cassie thought for a second. "I reserve the right to change my mind," she said, "but you're off the hook for now."

Nelson and Wi-Fi high-fived, trying not to shake the tablet too much and ruin the shot.

"Besides," Cassie added, "I was actually thinking of someone else."

Again, Miles's facial features kicked into high gear.

Again, his eyes went wide. But Cassie gave him no time for further protest.

"We need Mack," she said.

☙

The group didn't even need to check in with the camp office to know Mack's whereabouts. Instead, they left the ball-hockey court, crossed through senior camp, and skirted around the squat brown office toward the waterfront. The game was only six days away, after all, meaning they had less than no time to waste.

"I don't know if this is such a good idea," Miles said, sidling up to Cassie as they hustled down the hill. "Mack's already been through a lot this summer, and he slept on the lounge couch last night."

Cassie brushed off the idea with her hand. "That's exactly the point. He won't have to sleep on the couch if we win this. Besides, he could use something to do."

The two formed a group with Pat, Spike, and Mike, while Nelson and Wi-Fi trailed behind them, huddled together and talking into the tablet.

"Hey, guys!" Pat shouted back at them. "Watch your feet. Looks like someone's not cleaning up after their dog."

Nelson and Wi-Fi stopped dead, looking around and

checking the bottoms of their shoes. Then they shared a glance and looked back at the tablet screen.

"Vintage Pat!" Wi-Fi beamed.

The group continued on down the hill toward the lifeguard station.

"Does no one travel with counselors anymore?" groused Jama, the on-duty lifeguard, once they'd reached their destination.

"We're looking for Mack." Cassie scanned the waterfront. "Have you seen him?"

Jama pointed out to the water. A handful of kids in canoes were crisscrossing in front of an empty one floating aimlessly just off the shore. In the distance, Cassie could see lots of activity at the waterfront of Camp Clearwater.

"What?" she asked. "Did he swim across?"

Jama smiled and pointed more deliberately to Camp Average's own shoreline. "Look closer."

This time, she noticed that the empty canoe had a leg sticking out of it.

"He's in the canoe!" Cassie said. "But what's he doing?"

"I don't know. He just seemed kind of bummed." Jama shook his head. "But he signed up and put on a life jacket, so—"

"We sign up!" Cassie threw herself into the storage shed and almost immediately re-emerged with life jackets.

The properly attired crew shoved two canoes into the lake, with Cassie, Pat, and Miles in one, and Spike and Mike in the other. It didn't take them long to close in on their target.

"Mack!" shouted Cassie from the front of her canoe. "We're—"

"Going to ram you!" Pat shouted gleefully from the back of it.

Cassie realized that Pat was right. In their excitement, they had set their boats on a collision course.

"What?" Mack popped his head up just in time to see the canoes coming at him like torpedoes.

Cassie dug her paddle into the water to try to slow their progress, but it was too late.

"Uh..." said Mike.

"... oh," finished Spike, grabbing the sides of the canoe.

"Prepare for impact!" Pat squealed.

WHAM!

The two boats simultaneously hit Mack's flush on the side, pitching it forward ... and sending Mack right over the edge.

SPLASH!

"Man overboard!" Pat shrieked as the other paddlers turned to look.

"Hey!" Jama shouted from the lifeguard station. "No naval warfare!"

Mack's canoe righted itself, and when it stopped

rocking back and forth, Mack reached up with both hands to grab the side. His long brown hair was soaking wet and matted to his face, and his clothes were drenched. But his life jacket had kept him at the surface.

"Hey, guys," he said from the far side of the canoe, spitting out a stream of water. There was a distinct lack of surprise in his voice. "What's up?"

Cassie opened her mouth, but Pat got there first. "You should've seen it," he said. "We totally just rammed a canoe and sent this guy flying."

"I know," Mack said. "That was *me*."

"Yeah, but you didn't *see* it."

"Pat …" Cassie said.

"I always say," Pat continued, "pranks found are *so much* better than pranks earned."

"Pat!"

"Okay, okay!" He smacked his seat indignantly with an open hand. "We're sitting on a once-in-a-lifetime comedy gold mine here, but fine—go ahead and try to convince Mack to play ball hockey."

"PAT!"

This was not the way Cassie had seen the negotiation going. But when she scanned Mack's face for a reaction, he didn't seem put out, annoyed, or even interested. He just looked … blank.

"I can't play ball hockey," he said flatly.

"Neither can we," Pat said. "That's the problem."

"That's unfair," Cassie butted in. "Not to brag or anything, but I'm great—no, incredible. No, *stupendous*."

"We get ..." Mike started from his canoe.

"... the point," Spike finished.

"Did *you* get it?" Cassie asked Mack. "Because I'm *amazing*. And it's not just me. The twins are solid on defense, and Pat's good in net. Everyone knows a goalie can swing an entire game."

"That's true," Pat said, suddenly interested.

"What's true," Mack said, "is that I'd be no help to you. It's not that I'm no good—I'm not even experienced enough to be no good."

"How is that possible?" Cassie asked. "You're a good athlete. How could you never have played ball hockey?"

"I didn't say never." Mack shifted his hands on the side of the canoe as he bobbed in the water. "I played ... once."

Then he recounted the story of his first and only road-hockey experience, when he somehow jammed the stick between the road and his stomach at a dead run.

"I got winded so bad I passed out on the street," he said. "My friends had to get a neighbor to carry me home. Took a while to live it down. After that, I just kept my distance."

151

Cassie waited for Mack to finish speaking, then blew a raspberry. "Is that it?" She waved a hand in the air. "That's nothing. Miles is learning, too. You guys can do it together."

"In less than a week? Who's the coach?"

Cassie winced a little, betraying just a hint of doubt. "Laker," she said.

"Laker?!" Mack shouted. "He's a *baseball* coach! He might know less about ball hockey than I do!"

Cassie shrugged. "So we'll do the coaching."

Mack tilted his head back in frustration, then disappeared behind the far side of the canoe.

Cassie watched him dip out of sight, then abruptly stood and jumped out of her canoe into the water, shoes and all.

"Hey!" Miles shouted as Cassie's splash hit him.

"Woman overboard!" Pat exclaimed.

"Don't make me come in there, you guys!" Jama admonished. "One more outburst and you're done!"

Mack's head popped back up as Cassie swam around the bow of his canoe.

"I know this plan sounds crazy," she told him quietly. "But I also know it's a Camp Average plan. It's all wrong, but it's right all the same."

Cassie watched Mack squirm a little in the water. She

realized he had rarely been on this side of this kind of talk.

"A Camp Average plan without Mack is like a ball-hockey game without a ball," she pressed. "It doesn't work."

"What doesn't work?" Pat whispered from behind Cassie. Evidently, he had slipped into the water after her. "What are you guys talking about?"

"*Pat!*" shouted the entire crew.

"THAT'S IT!" Jama shouted. "Everybody out of the water!"

Miles and Spike and Mike paddled their canoes to shore, while Cassie, Pat, and Mack followed along by pushing his.

They were nearly back when Mack finally spoke. "If you really think you need me," he said solemnly, "I'm in."

Cassie beamed. "Thanks," she said, touching her feet down. She grabbed the bow of the canoe and pulled it onto land. "You probably won't regret this." She thought for a second, then added, "Very much."

Mack smiled sadly. "Truth is, I could use something to take my mind off things," he said. He locked eyes with Miles as they helped Cassie drag the canoe onto the beach. "I tried to video call Andre a dozen times this morning. No answer. They could have taken his tablet or put him

153

on solo croquet-pitch duty or …" Mack shook his head. "I don't want to think about it. And in the meantime," he said, his face brightening, "I know someone who'll actually be able to help."

CHAPTER 20

"*THAT'S* THINKING LIKE A GOLFER"

The hockey stick felt foreign in Mack's hands as he stood in the middle of the ball-hockey court with the rest of his new team after lunch. It had a black wooden shaft and an orange plastic blade, and he was holding it away from his body like it was a deadly weapon that could go off at any time.

"Looking … good, Mack," Cassie encouraged.

Mack had heard that same tone of voice before. Only it had been Laker speaking that way to Cassie's brother when he was trying baseball for the first time. Back then, Nelson didn't know the batter's box from the backstop—and now, to Mack's chagrin, that was him learning ball hockey.

"So," Cassie continued, "where's this help you promised?"

"I'm sure she's on the way," Mack said. He tried to put his weight on the stick, but the blade buckled against the concrete court and sent him sprawling sideways. "She's usually very prompt."

Just then, the kids on the court began to make out the faint sound of two voices in heated debate. After a moment, the arguing drew closer. After another, Nicole and Makayla rounded the edge of the nearest cabin and walked swiftly toward the court.

"I'm telling you," Makayla said loudly enough for all to hear, "ball hockey is nothing like golf."

Nicole rolled her eyes. "What shape is a golf ball?"

"It's round."

"And what shape is a ball-hockey ball?"

"They're both round!" Makayla exploded.

"And what does a putter look like?" Nicole asked, undeterred.

"You want me to say it looks like a hockey stick."

"Because it *does* look like a hockey stick! The two games are basically the same!"

Nicole dragged Makayla over the boards and out to join the group. They now formed a loose eight-person circle around the court's center dot, with another three—Nelson, Wi-Fi, and a perpetually dozing Laker—in the stands nearby.

"Hi," said Nicole, elbowing her friend lightly in the ribs.

"Hey," added Makayla, a sour look on her face.

For a second, no one—not even Cassie—said anything. Maybe it was because Mack's invite had resulted in yet another player who had no interest in playing?

Then Miles jumped in to fill the awkward silence. He had a small dog-eared paperback called *For Those About to Hock: The Complete Guide to Ball Hockey* in his hand.

"Actually," he began, "other than what Nicole just said, I don't think there are *any* similarities between the two sports."

Nicole glowered at her friend from back home. "Oh, *really*, Miles?" she said.

He didn't seem to notice her threatening tone. "Yes, really," he said, picking up steam. "Unlike golf, ball hockey is a team sport—played with five players and one goalie per side—and the aim is to accumulate the highest score, not the lowest. There are no tee boxes or sand traps or water hazards, and no one waits politely for you to take a shot unless there's been a penalty on a breakaway or the game's gone to a shoot-out."

Makayla shot a withering sideways look at Nicole and crossed her arms in an I-told-you-so pose.

"In fact," Miles continued, "ball hockey even has a few differences from ice hockey … beyond, you know, the lack of ice."

157

This was news to Mack, who cocked an eyebrow.

But Nicole was only growing angrier. "Do tell," she said sarcastically.

Again, Miles missed the tone. He cracked the book and scanned a page near the beginning.

"Many of the rules are the same, but teams in most ball-hockey leagues play two twenty-minute halves instead of three twenty-minute periods, as in the NHL," he said. "Teams are generally smaller and shifts are longer. Also, a ball will curve when shot in ways a puck won't."

Miles looked up from his book and finally caught Nicole's glare. His eyes darted from her to Makayla and back.

Then he cleared his throat apologetically. "Or so I've read."

While Miles shifted awkwardly from foot to foot and fiddled with the tag on the neck of his T-shirt, the other kids again fell into an awkward silence. Mack watched Cassie, who, he realized, was watching him.

Then he figured out what was going on.

Though he'd never really asked for the job, rallying reluctant troops had become Mack's thing. And he knew from experience how hard it was to stand at the front of a group and say, "I know what to do"—especially when you weren't sure you were right. He realized Cassie didn't need his vote of confidence, but he also realized it couldn't hurt.

"What's next, boss?" he asked.

Cassie clenched her teeth, swallowed hard, and nodded. "Right," she said. "Time to see what we've got!" She turned to the bleachers. "Laker?" she asked, projecting her voice.

The coach grunted, half asleep, and rolled awkwardly onto his side. Now he was lying with his right hip on one bench seat and the side of his head on the one above it. His upper body kind of sagged into the gap between them.

"That doesn't look good for his neck," said Nicole.

"No," Pat said, stepping between her and Makayla, "but that's golf, right?"

Nicole didn't move a muscle.

"I mean, we can all agree taking a nap is basically the same thing as golf," he said, backing away.

Nicole blinked. It was the most menacing blink Mack had ever seen.

"Pat," she said calmly as the boy broke into a run, "I'm going to hurt you."

"*That's* thinking like a golfer!" he called over his shoulder as he reached his net and began to put on his goalie equipment. "You're going to fit right in!"

Cassie directed Nicole and Makayla to her stash of

gear, then handed each a stick. "So how much experience do you two have?"

Nicole answered by lifting a ball off the court with the blade of her stick. She bounced the ball there a few times, then batted it out of the air. It screamed across the court and settled into the bottom left corner of the net where Pat was currently dressing.

"Hey!" he yelled. "Wait'll I get my pads on!"

Cassie turned to Nicole, her mouth wide open. "Why didn't you come this morning?"

"We had croquet practice," Nicole said. "I'm kind of falling in love with that sport."

"I'm *not* falling in love with it," Makayla chimed in. "And I've just played a little ball hockey in gym class."

Once Pat finished donning his helmet, chest protector, glove, blocker, and boxy leg pads, Cassie lined everyone up behind the blue line to practice slap shots.

She went first, rifling a shot to Pat's glove side.

Then Spike and Mike fired at the same time.

"No fair!" Pat said as Spike's shot squeezed into the space between his feet. "Right through the five-hole," he grumbled.

Makayla's shot was surprisingly powerful, and Nicole's was so sharp it made ball hockey look like her best sport (not just one of the top fifteen or so).

Miles had textbook form—not surprisingly, since he'd learned it from a textbook—even if the shot itself lacked oomph.

When it was finally Mack's turn, he gripped the stick like a baseball bat. Then he lifted it back behind his head, brought it down with a fury ... and missed the ball entirely, swinging way wide of it.

His cheeks reddened, and he looked around at the other kids to see if they'd been watching.

They had.

"Try again," Cassie encouraged him. "And this time, move your right hand down the stick a bit. You get more control that way."

"Oh," he said, trying out the new grip. "Right."

Again Mack took aim at the ball. He held the stick with his hands apart as Cassie had suggested, lifted the blade high behind him, and brought it quickly back down.

This time he caught just the top of the ball, sending it dribbling toward Pat, who let it roll softly into his goalie stick.

"Almost got me," Pat said with a smile.

"Thanks," Mack replied with a death stare.

He walked around to the back of the line, determined to watch his new teammates for pointers. When it was his turn again, he was sure he had the mechanics down.

"Let's see it, Mack," Cassie said.

He separated his hands on the stick, lined up the ball on its blade, wound up, and let fly. This time he sent the ball flying—straight out to the left and over the boards. It rolled to a stop in the grass about fifty feet away from its starting point.

"Nice form," said Nicole.

"Good contact," added Makayla.

Spike and Mike mumbled encouragement.

But no one laughed.

Mack had missed the net about as badly as you could miss it—save for maybe smacking the ball backward. He knew his friends well enough to be sure that if they believed he could do any better, they would've felt more than comfortable making fun of his shot. In that light, their kind words landed like daggers. He would've preferred to have Pat wave both hands in the air and shout, "Hey, man—net's over here."

Or Nicole crow about how she was better than him at this sport, too.

No such luck, he thought.

Their silence made one thing painfully clear: somehow, impossibly, Mack was even worse at this than he thought he'd be.

He walked to the back of the line to stew while his

teammates continued taking normal-looking slap shots. Then he felt a hand on his shoulder.

"Don't worry, buddy," Cassie said, reading his thoughts. "You'll pick it up when we scrimmage."

Mack turned and dropped his chin to his chest so he could look her in the eye. "I don't know about—"

"Wait!" Miles said, cutting him off. "Did you say scrimmage?"

CHAPTER 21

"I TAKE OFFENSE IN ADVANCE"

"Are you sure this is a good idea?" Miles asked Cassie from the bench as she walked onto the court. Like everyone else on the team, she'd donned a white helmet with a full face cage as well as a pair of padded black hockey gloves.

"Totally," Cassie said, turning back to him and running in place to warm up. "I mean, we've got at least two people who have no idea what they're doing."

"That was going to be my point," Miles replied, not in the least offended that she meant him.

He looked at Mack, who was standing on their team's blue line. He was holding his stick up and knocking it lightly against his helmet's face cage—apparently testing for structural integrity.

Cassie followed his gaze. "I just figured the best way to get comfortable is to play." She nodded toward the other end of the court. "And our opponents promised to take it easy on us."

This time, Miles followed Cassie's gaze. The rest of their campmates had been either too disinterested or too scared of Garth to help. So Cassie had bypassed kids and gathered a group of the nearest and most willing adults she could find, telling them only that her team was prepping for a big game—not that cabin 23 was at stake. And now, those adults were all stretching out their limbs to get ready for the scrimmage.

Standing near the center line were Hassan, the junior baseball coach, and basketball coaches Brian and Tamara. And back toward the net were lifeguard Jama and camp director Cheryl.

As calm, reasonable, and supportive as Miles knew these five to be—they had all helped him and his friends in one way or another the past two summers—they sure seemed intimidating in their face cages and gloves that made their hands look like Incredible Hulk fists.

In goal was a yawning Laker, bending over at the waist under the weight of his head-to-toe padding.

"All good, Coach?" Cassie shouted at him. "Any last words of wisdom?"

Laker gave her a weary thumbs-up. "Give 'em ... er, *us* heck," he said flatly. "We won't know what hit us."

Cassie waved in her teammates. "You heard him," she said once everyone had formed a huddle. "The

Hortonians will have more skill than us, so we have to play faster and harder. But we also have to protect our own end. Defense, make sure you stay home."

Mack put up his hand. "I'm on defense, right?"

"With your shot?" Cassie asked, forgetting herself. Then coughed. "Yes, you're on defense." She handed him the depth chart she had scrawled onto a scrap of white paper.

FIRST FORWARD LINE	NICOLE, CASSIE, MAKAYLA
FORWARD SUB	MILES
FIRST DEFENSE LINE	SPIKE, MIKE
DEFENSE SUB	MACK
GOALIE	PAT
GOALIE SUB	DON'T GET INJURED, PAT!!!

"Okay, cool," Mack said, holding the paper in front of him with glazed eyes. "Where's home?"

"Just stay close to the net and play defense!"

"Oh!" Mack said. "Right. I can do that."

"That's the spirit," Cassie told him. Then to everyone else, she said, "We've got two subs, so make sure to keep rotating in and out. Make sense?"

Everyone nodded.

Cassie grinned and thrust her hand forward. "On three!" she shouted. "One, two, three ..."

"AVERAGE!"

Miles watched Mack's face as the two sat down on the bench to start the game. It looked like his friend wanted to ask a question but was tamping it down. And then Miles realized that they hadn't worked on defense at all. In the little practice time they'd had, they'd focused only on shooting. Mack's experience staying between a player and the hoop in basketball would come in handy, but everything else he'd have to figure out on the fly.

"Uh, Cassie?" Miles called to his team captain. "Maybe we—"

But he didn't get to finish his sentence.

Simon Yang, the senior-camp director who had offered to ref the game, walked to center court holding up an orange ball. "Game on!" he shouted.

☙

Simon dropped the ball between Jama and Cassie, whose quick reflexes let her poke out the blade of her stick and pull the ball back to Nicole, waiting behind her.

Nicole quickly passed it ahead to Makayla on the right wing, while Cassie kept pace down the middle of the court. Spike and Mike trailed the play, careful to stay on their own half of the court as Cassie had instructed.

Makayla corralled the ball along the boards near the blue line, stopped, and turned as Cheryl ran toward her.

"I'm open!" shouted Cassie.

Makayla exuded a sense of calm—she had seen her fair share of defensive pressure on the basketball court. Still, her pass to Cassie went right into Cheryl's outstretched stick, and the ball became an orange blur as it ricocheted off toward center court.

"Get back!" yelled Cassie, screeching her sneakers to a stop and pivoting to her own end.

Jama picked up the ball on the rush and barreled down toward the kids' net. Proving to be a whiz with a hockey stick, the lifeguard split between Spike and Mike to fire a shot to the top right corner of the net.

Pat shot his left leg to the side and whipped his gloved left hand out into space.

THWIP!

The ball settled into the glove an inch from the net.

"Way to go, Pat!" Miles shouted from the bench.

"Nice save!" cheered Mack.

Pat playfully tossed the ball to himself and caught it again as the adults retreated. Then he dropped the ball to the side of his net as Mike circled around the back of it. Mike got the ball on his stick and charged forward, passing ahead to Nicole down the left boards.

Miles followed the ball as it went down the court. Then he felt a rush of air on his right side. He turned his head to find Spike sitting beside him, working hard to catch his breath.

"What are you doing here?!" Miles shouted at him. "Aren't you supposed to be playing?"

"I'm subbing ..." Spike started to say before trailing off. He looked to the empty bench beside him. "Oh, right!" he said, evidently unused to finishing his own sentences. "I'm subbing off!"

"Already?!"

"That's how it works." Spike pointed at the court and looked desperately at his teammates on the bench. "Get in there, Mack. We're playing shorthanded!"

Miles looked up and discovered Spike was right. Including goalies, five of his teammates were playing against six adults.

"Mack," Miles said to his friend.

But Mack, seemingly entranced by the ball, didn't move.

"Mack!" Miles shouted. "You're on!"

Mack stood abruptly, a panicked look on his face. He threw his right leg over the boards like he was mounting a horse and kicked Spike in the calf in the process.

"Ow!" Spike shouted.

"Sorry!" Mack said. Then he pulled his left leg over after him ... and kicked Spike a second time.

"OW!"

Mack got both feet underneath him on the court just in time to watch Hassan race past him. Evidently Mack's teammates had turned the ball over at the other end, and their opponents were now in the process of driving it down their throats.

"Let's go, Mack!" called Cassie. "You're supposed to be on defense!"

"I'm trying to be!"

Mack chased after Hassan, who had a good five-step head start, two teammates to pass to, and only one defender between him and the goal.

Backpedaling toward his own net, Mike suddenly lunged forward to try to poke the ball away from Hassan with his stick. But the junior baseball coach deftly passed sideways to Tamara on the run. Suddenly, Tamara and Brian had a two-on-none breakaway. Ten feet away from the net, with her dark hair bouncing behind her, Tamara faked a shot to Pat's left, then slapped one low and to his right.

Luckily for Mack and the others, Pat wasn't so easily tricked. He kept his balance during the shot fake, then dropped to his knees to block Tamara's actual shot.

"Nice one, Pat!" Mack shouted, stopping in place.

But the play wasn't over. The ball ricocheted off Pat's pads toward Brian. He directed it to Hassan, who tapped it into the other side of the goal before Pat could dive across.

"Yes!" Tamara shouted.

Hassan ran around the back of the goal, a smile on his face, then tapped Pat's pads with his stick.

"Not your fault," Hassan told him. "You're on fire."

Miles watched from the bench as Mack took this in. He was standing on his team's own blue line, and most of his opponents were closer to his net than he was.

If it wasn't the goalie's fault, that meant it had to be …

"Don't worry about it, Mack," Nicole said, patting him on the shoulder. "It's just like basketball. Play's not over until we get the rebound. You'll get it."

Evidence of that didn't immediately arrive, however. Miles and Spike subbed in for Makayla and Mike, and the new lineup quickly found itself in trouble again. This time, Mack was standing in the right spot—near his own net, ready to steal the ball and pass it to a teammate—but he got easily deked by Brian. Pat blocked three shots before finally diving on the ball and gaining possession for his team.

"Mack!" Mike yelled from the sideline. "Shift change!"

Miles watched Mack breathe a sigh of relief as he

sprinted to the sideline and leapt over the boards, making way for Mike to join the fray.

Though Miles wanted to ignore it, he immediately felt a change. With two solid defenders behind them, he, Cassie, and Makayla—who had come back in for Nicole—ran up court with a new confidence. After all, if they turned the ball over, they were in good hands.

Setting the adults back on their heels, the kids pushed swiftly ahead. The ball pinged from Cassie to Miles to Makayla as they closed in on the net. Finally, Miles ducked underneath Jama's arm near the crease—the half-circle area around the goalie—and tapped in a pass from Makayla for the team's first point.

"All …" shouted Mike from the other end of the court.

"… right!" followed Spike.

"Miles!" Cassie grabbed him by the shoulder. "You know what you're doing!"

Miles shrugged. "I read a book," he said. "The highest-percentage scoring opportunities come from the slot."

"Whatever!" Cassie said. "You're a natural."

Miles ran back down to his own end and fist-bumped the players on the bench without slowing down. (He'd read about that tradition in his book, too.)

"Great shot, Miles," Mack said, smiling when his friend passed by.

"Now it's our turn to make some highlights," Nicole told Mack, her face a mask of determination as she left the bench. "We're on."

Immediately, Mack's smile disappeared. He took the court and watched Nicole win a face-off with Brian. But before he knew it, the opposing team had stolen the ball and was coming at him again.

With shaky hands, he ran to intercept Tamara, but she got rid of the ball before he got there—and then flew by him as he tried in vain to slow his momentum. He turned and chased Jama, the new ball carrier, who immediately fired crosscourt to Brian.

"Come on!" Mack shouted.

Then he got a stroke of luck. Brian wired a wrist shot at the net, but Pat easily turned it away with his blocker. The ball rebounded all the way out to Mack.

"Got it!" he said gleefully.

He planted the blade of his stick on the ground to stop the ball. But the ball bounced right off it—and back toward his own net.

Tamara gathered the ball and fired yet another shot at Pat, who dropped to his knees to block it with his chest protector.

"Sub!" shouted Mack, already out of breath. "Sub!"

"It's not your turn!" admonished Mike, Mack's

defensive linemate, as he tried to put himself between the ball and the net.

"And we can't change when we're on defense anyway!" added Cassie from the bench.

The shift lasted for what seemed like hours, with the adults taking shot after shot before—finally, mercifully—Mike stripped Brian of the ball and passed it out of their zone. Then he wheezed his way to the bench to switch spots with his twin brother.

For the next half hour, the game went on like that—Mack's team dominating play when he was on the bench and getting dominated when he wasn't.

On his third shift: Mack spent about thirty seconds defending the wrong goal.

On his fifth shift: Mack set up so close to Pat that he completely blocked his friend's view. The ball whipped by them both and settled into the net unseen.

On his eighth shift: Mack forgot to bring his stick onto the court. It took a while for him to realize it, though, because Pat kept yelling at him about his "lumber."

After Mack's tenth shift, the dinner bell rang out through the loudspeakers stationed around camp.

"Okay, let's call it," Laker shouted.

"Who won?" asked Mack, roughly depositing his stick

and the rest of his equipment back where he had found them.

"Oh, I don't think anyone was keeping track," said Cheryl from across the court, her hands on her knees.

Mack turned to Miles. "Really?"

Miles had a head for numbers—and everything else, actually. Even without his score sheets in front of him, he could've rhymed off how many goals and assists each player on both teams had accumulated.

"The adults won," Miles said reluctantly. "Six to four."

For a moment, there was silence.

Sure, the kids had faced off against a team of adults, but none of those adults even pretended to be a serious ball-hockey player. Even worse, they hadn't had any subs, and now that they were removing their gear, it was clear how exhausted they were.

Hassan looked around at the kids' long faces. "Quick question," he said. "Are you guys crazy?"

That got their attention.

"This was essentially your first *practice*, and you did great. You got your lines working, and you put the ball in the net. Cassie's a great captain, and the rest of you really fed off her energy."

Nicole threw her arm around Cassie, who beamed.

"Plus, no offense to Laker ..." Hassan continued.

Laker crossed his arms. "I take offense in advance."

"But if we had switched goalies, the score would have been way more lopsided. Pat's awesome."

"I was right to take offense," Laker said. "Offense taken."

Pat gave an aw-shucks wave as his teammates patted him on the back. Then he put his hand up for a high five with Laker, who pretended not to notice.

"And you," Hassan said, looking at Mack, "you can only—" He stopped himself with a cough, then gestured to the whole group. "Your *new players* can only improve, and with them so will your defense."

Mack said nothing to that. But with one look at his downcast eyes and slack mouth, Miles knew: he didn't believe Hassan in the slightest. If Mack was going to help the team, Miles thought, he would need some help of his own.

Miles looked at Pat, who was holding his nose as he took off his hockey gear; at Cassie, who was shaking a fist at Nelson and Wi-Fi in the stands; at Nicole and Makayla, who still had brambles in their hair from the overnight camping trip two nights earlier.

The words repeated inside Miles's brain: if Mack was going to help the team, he would need some help of his own. He would need his friends.

All his friends.

And right then, Miles knew what he had to do.

CHAPTER
22

"GUESS WE'RE GOING CAMPING"

Mack hung around the court just long enough to make it seem like he was okay with how the game had gone—and in particular, with the way he had played.

Which, of course, wasn't true.

He bumped a few more fists, then hopped over the boards to head to dinner. But he didn't get far before walking right into the path of a large group of Hortonia campers—Garth among them.

"Oh no," he muttered, slowing his pace as he suddenly flashed back to his last conversation with Garth, two summers earlier. "Here we go."

Just when it seemed like the hulking broken-nosed boy was going to turn his gaze up the path, though, Alexei walked between them. Mack didn't know whether he'd done it on purpose, but Alexei stayed there—a fixed object blocking Garth's view—until the group had turned a corner and ambled off to the mess hall.

"Huh," Mack said, watching them go.

Just then, Miles ran into view, obliviously moving against the current of Hortonians.

Mack frowned, confused, as his friend stopped in front of him. "Weren't you just at the ball-hockey court?" he asked. "Where'd you come from?"

"The office."

Miles's mouth suddenly morphed into a knowing smirk—as if they were watching a movie, and only he knew what was going to happen next. It was a look Mack had seen on Pat's face dozens of times.

"And ... ?"

"I signed us up for the overnight camping trip," Miles blurted excitedly.

Mack furrowed his brow. "What?" he asked. This was their seventh year at Camp Average, and they hadn't gone on the overnight trip since they were mini campers. "Why?"

"One, you have no bed in our cabin, so you're not really sacrificing a night of comfort."

"True."

"And two, I just need you to trust me."

Mack thought for a second. There were two or three people he trusted as much as Miles—Andre, for one; his parents, on their good days—but there was no one in the world he trusted *more*.

"Okay." He shrugged. "Guess we're going camping."

Mack followed Miles back to cabin 23, where they grabbed their darkest jogging pants and hoodies—Miles said black was a requirement—and their sleeping bags. Then they left the cabin as quickly as they'd come. And while the bulk of their campmates walked to the mess hall in the late-day sun, the two boys veered off to the camp office to meet the rest of their group.

But they had a tail.

Mack heard footsteps thumping closer at top speed, and he and Miles turned.

"Pat?" Miles asked, suddenly worried.

"If you think I'm sleeping in that cabin with Forehead when you're not there, you're crazy," Pat said, falling in with them. "I'm going with you."

"B-but," Miles said, stammering. "But you can't. You haven't signed up."

"When has that ever stopped us before? I'll sign up when I get there."

"But you're not in your ... darkest hoodie."

Pat looked down at his outfit. He was decked out in an orange camp T-shirt and a floral-print zip-up sweatshirt with red shorts.

"I think I'll manage," he said.

Mack watched with interest as Miles hyperventilated

and clenched his fists. It was clear Pat's presence was throwing a wrench in whatever plans he'd made, but Mack didn't know enough about those plans to figure out why.

"No, you—" Miles used the thumb and middle finger of his right hand to pinch his entire forehead at the temples. "Fine. You're just staying in your own tent."

෬෧

As it turned out, Pat would not be staying in his own tent. He'd had no trouble signing up for the overnight trip, but space was at a premium. The tents held three campers apiece, so it only made sense for friends Mack, Miles, and Pat to bunk together.

Also, everyone else was afraid of falling asleep next to Pat and waking up with one hand in a bowl of water.

"Harsh," Pat said when Hassan, one of the two counselors in charge, told them this over a dinner of hot dogs and baked beans. "Where would I even get a bowl?"

"I get it, Pat, but reputations can be—"

"No, seriously," Pat said. "Where would I get one, should I find the need?"

The overnighter always took place in a clearing at the highest point of the campground. It was surrounded by densely packed trees, which provided both the desired feeling of isolation and the branches needed for cooking s'mores over the fire.

Soon the s'mores had been eaten and the ghost stories had been told, and it was time for lights-out. Five minutes later, Pat was snoring. Mack watched Miles lean over their sleeping friend, eyes wide, as if watching the evenness of his breaths. He even lightly poked Pat, who didn't stir.

Satisfied, Miles sat up and locked eyes with Mack.

"We're leaving," he whispered.

Mack had a sudden sense of déjà vu. He had heard those words before in a situation just like this. But he'd heard them from himself.

"We're ... huh?" Mack scratched his head. "Where are we leaving to?"

"Shh!" Miles said. "I'll explain on the way."

"The way to where?"

"SHHHHH!"

Miles unzipped the front flap of the tent and poked his head out. There were five other tents in view—three full of kids, and two solo ones containing a single counselor each. Soft white light emanated from inside the counselor tents.

"Good," Miles whispered. "They're distracted. A herd of wild buffalo could walk by my parents when they're looking at their phones, and they wouldn't hear a thing. Let's go."

Miles ducked noiselessly through the flap and crouch-walked through the minefield of tents across the clearing. Mack took a deep breath and followed.

Once outside, the air felt colder and wetter than it had even a few minutes before, when they'd settled in for the night. Mack pulled his hood over his head and yanked on the strings to tighten it, then zipped his sweatshirt up to the top.

It was a clear night, and Mack could see by the light of the moon as he crossed the clearing. Still, he almost tripped over a counselor's tent line and came a single step from walking into the campfire pit—either of which would've botched the plan, whatever it was.

After a few more moments, Mack met Miles at the far edge of the clearing. They were well away from the tents now, and before them was a group of tall oak trees.

"Follow me," Miles said at normal volume.

"But …"

His friend was already gone, though, swallowed up by the darkness of the woods.

The two passed as quickly as possible around the trees and through the shrubbery, using only the blue-green backlight from Miles's watch to guide them. On several occasions, branches hit Mack across the face—Miles was too small to warn him against them.

"A guy really *could* get poison ivy doing something like this," Mack mumbled.

Then, just as suddenly as they'd entered the woods, they found themselves beyond them. They scurried down one side of a dry, shallow ditch and up the other onto the gravel shoulder of the road, where Miles took a sharp right and started walking. There were telephone poles and lines running alongside the road but no streetlights.

As the two boys trudged along shoulder to shoulder, they were bathed not just in darkness but in silence. It was so quiet on the little-used back road that Mack felt like his senses were dulled. Finally, he could take the suspense no more.

"Where are we going?"

"I told you I'd explain on the way," Miles said. "I'm just figuring out how to—"

Just then, they heard a noise from the underbrush.

Mack stopped dead and grabbed Miles by the shoulder.

"Was that you?" he asked.

"I hoped it was *you*," Miles peeped.

The two boys turned their heads on petrified neck muscles to look at each other, then pivoted toward the side of the road … to find Pat. He was dressed in the same bright clothes as before, and even in the darkness, he stood out like a neon sign.

"Pat!" Miles whisper-shouted. "I thought you were asleep!"

"Pretty good, eh?" He smiled proudly. "I was only pretending to be asleep so *you guys* would go to sleep and then I could ..."

Mack raised an eyebrow. "Then you could what?"

"Not finish that sentence."

"If you were awake, why didn't you just follow us when we left?"

"And ruin my big entrance?" Pat scoffed. "The hairs on your necks stood up so fast they nearly poked my eyes out! It was awesome."

Miles fumed. He threw up his hands and walked a tight circle.

"So anyway," Pat said, rocking nonchalantly on his heels, "where did you say we're going?"

"You're not going anywhere but back to the tent," Miles said in a huff.

"Miles," Pat admonished, "Mack shouldn't have to leave. Besides, wouldn't someone stumbling back into the campsite create more risk of getting caught?"

Miles clenched his jaw and pursed his lips. Then he looked at Mack, who raised his hands, trying to stay out of it.

"Fine. You can come," Miles said, "to Killington."

CHAPTER
23

"THIS IS ME
MAKING AMENDS"

"But you *hate* plans like this!" Mack said for what felt like the hundredth time. "If we get caught—"

"You don't need to tell me what happens."

Miles knew the consequences of sneaking off in the middle of the night. If they were caught, they could get kicked out of camp. Even worse, if their counselors discovered their empty tent, they'd be scared to death.

Miles didn't like thinking about any of that. But still, he felt like they were doing the right thing.

"If my math is right, we're almost there," he said.

"Again, though," Pat said, "*why* are we almost there?"

The trio had been walking for over an hour. Other than the handful of times they had dived into the ditch to avoid being seen by an oncoming vehicle, Mack and Pat had spent the entire trek prodding Miles for answers.

"We're finishing what we started," he said finally.

"When Andre insisted on honoring his deal and spending the summer at Killington, Mack made sure he wouldn't be alone."

Miles looked at his friend, who shrugged modestly.

"I thought I could go one better," he said, "and get you both out of there without compromising Andre's word. But I just got one of you out. I wrecked your plan and left Andre stranded there, enduring who knows what kind of torment."

"That wasn't your fault," Mack said.

Miles dropped his eyes to the ground. "I think it was," he said. "And so, this is me making amends. Just because you're not there, that doesn't mean you can't show Andre you're not still *there*."

"That makes sense," said Pat. "And at the same time, no sense at all."

Miles's nostrils flared. He stepped into Pat's personal space. "One, I never asked you to come! Not that I didn't want you along—I just didn't want to risk getting anyone else in trouble. And two, we're helping our friend!" He raised a finger up above his head so it was an inch away from his friend's nose. "Got it?"

Pat stepped back. "Yes," he said. "Sir?"

Miles jerked a thumb over his shoulder. "Should be just around this bend."

He took off at a fast walk along the road. But when they rounded the curve to the left and emerged onto a straight stretch, there was no camp entrance in sight.

Just road and trees and sky and stars.

Miles cast a sideways glance at Mack and could see the worry on his face.

"This is unbelievably cool of you, Miles," Mack said. "But …"

"But what?"

"When we get to the front gate, there's a long narrow driveway. And lights. And adults." Mack rubbed his upper arm, inadvertently hugging himself. "How are we going to get in without being seen?"

"The same way we got out of Camp Average," Miles replied. "Through the woods."

Mack furrowed his brow.

"You said the Mendoza building butts onto a wooded area, right?"

"Right."

"And you could hear trucks through the window sometimes, right?"

"Right."

"Well, that's because you were"—Miles stopped abruptly, pointing at the woods—"right through here."

Mack raised an eyebrow. "How do you know?"

Miles pointed up. The sky was lit up like a baseball stadium, which is what Killington essentially was.

"The lights begin about here, and the gates aren't coming up for nearly another half mile. That means this must be the back edge of the left side of camp. Or in other words—"

"Right where my dorm was."

"Exactly."

Mack shook his head in admiration. "Exactly," he repeated.

CHAPTER
24

"DON'T FREAK OUT"

Again the boys passed through the dry ditch by the road-side. To Mack's surprise, the woods on the other side of it were narrower than the ones at Camp Average. It took only a minute to pass through and emerge next to the Mendoza building.

"Nice place." Pat craned his neck to take in the plain-looking dorm. "Real homey."

Mack poked his head around the front edge of the building. "Meh," he whispered. "It grows on you."

Miles checked his watch. "It's after eleven," he said with a sense of urgency. "Where to, Mack?"

"Follow me."

The boys crept past the Dietrich, Koufax, and Mays buildings—stopping often to look for coaches or dorm supervisors—before arriving at Andre's dorm. They cracked the door, slipped inside, and closed it behind them.

Mack held his index finger against his lips.

"Yeah, like we were going to start making jokes," Pat whispered. Then he thought for a second and added, "Other than that one."

Mack led them down the hall to the door marked 1B and ushered his companions inside. They closed the door softly behind them, then looked around the room. Or tried to. The blinds were drawn, and it might as well have been the bottom of an ink-black ocean.

"Stay here," Mack whispered, reaching out to pat each of his friends on the shoulder.

He moved through the room carefully, delicately, by memory, until his extended arms butted into the end of Andre's four-poster bed. He felt his way along the side and knelt by the headboard.

"Hey, man, wake up," Mack whispered, reaching out in front of him to poke his friend's shoulder. "And don't freak out."

Suddenly, a bright white light burst forth in front of him, illuminating the face of the boy in the bed.

Who wasn't Andre.

"Wha—?!" Mack fell backward, his butt hitting the ground with a thud.

They were in Andre's room, but Andre wasn't here. It was Reo, and he had fallen asleep with his tablet lying open on his chest, as always.

Suddenly they heard someone pounding on the wall.

"Keep it down, Reo!" shouted a deep and muffled voice.

"Abort!" Mack whispered, turning to leave. But ironically, the pounding and shouting for Reo to keep it down was what finally woke Reo up.

"Mack?" he said groggily. Then again, a little more loudly: "Mack?!"

"Shhhh!" Mack whispered. "Deets will hear!"

"That was Deets?!" Miles peeped.

In the wan light from the tablet, Mack could see his friend turn green, suddenly mortified by the risks of his own plan.

"What are you doing here?" Reo croaked.

Mack had to think about that. "We … er, came for a visit," he said finally. Then he furrowed his brow. "What are *you* doing here? What happened to Andre? Did he—"

Reo raised his hands. "Cool it, okay?" he whispered. "Everything's fine. After you left, Andre told us he felt bad about getting the best room. We're on a rotation. Tonight's my night."

Pat scratched his head. "So then where's Andre?"

"Mendoza."

Five minutes later, the boys were breaking and entering their second room of the night. Only this time, Mack was using Miles's watch as a flashlight and there were four of them—Reo had come along.

Mack opened the door quietly, careful not to hit the bedframe inside, then slipped in. Pat followed, then Reo. Miles was just about to enter when he saw someone come out of the bathroom down the hall. He jumped into the room, knocking the door against the bedframe, then slammed it shut behind him.

As Andre bolted upright in what had been Reo's bed, Mack turned back toward the door, raised the watch high in the air, and turned the light on Miles, who was breathing hard and whispering to himself.

"Please don't let there be a knock at the door. Please don't let there be a—"

There was a knock at the door.

The noise made Miles leap forward a few inches—just enough to bump into Reo, who fell onto the backs of Pat's legs, forcing him to headbutt Mack in the chest.

Mack sprawled backward, throwing his hands behind him and grabbing at whatever he could find. Unfortunately, it ended up being the room's vertical blinds, which he pulled right out of the window frame with a manic clatter.

As the boys scattered, the door flew open. House stomped into the room and smacked the light switch.

"What's going on?!"

"House!" Andre blurted, scanning the chaos around him in what appeared to be a mixture of surprise and terror and delight. "This isn't ... what it looks like?"

House's eyes widened. The room should've held just Andre and Benny (who was in his usual top bunk, and, like his roommate, looking wildly about). But there were also two boys House didn't recognize standing flat against the wall behind the bunk bed—not to mention two running shoes and attached ankles poking out from under it.

Meanwhile, another boy sat against the far wall, covered head to toe in beige vertical blinds.

Mack looked out from the spaces between the blinds at his old dorm supervisor. He knew what was at stake here. This was a man who'd been derailed from his fast-rising Killington coaching career by the very boys now scattered around the room. Were he to turn in the three uninvited guests, he would effectively send them home for the summer. Maybe for *the rest of* their summers. He would become a favorite not just of Deets but of the Camp Killington directors as well—he would be the coach who caught those Camp Average kids trying to mess with their players.

Mack waited to see how he would react. They all did.

A few seconds passed. Then, little by little, House's eyes returned to their normal state of openness. His breathing slowed.

"It's okay, Andre," he said rather loudly. "You were just … uh, sleepwalking."

Andre let out a deep breath. "Sleepwalking," he said, getting House's meaning. "Yeah, right. Sorry! Gotta watch that."

"Also, in case it wasn't clear," House said, nodding at Mack, "you need to be done *sleepwalking* in, like, two minutes."

"Got it," Andre said.

"Or the … um, sandman will get you."

Pat poked his head out from behind the bunk bed. "Wait, are we still talking about us sneaking in? Or does Andre need to see some sort of paranormal sleep specialist?"

House stared him down. Then he chuckled despite himself. "Where do they find you guys?" he asked.

He exited the room and pulled the door closed, leaving the light on. The boys listened to his footsteps recede down the hallway, and heard his door open and close. Then, at last, there was silence.

"What are you doing here?!" Andre whispered, leaping like a cat to help Mack out of the blinds.

"They came for a visit," said Reo, pushing himself out from underneath the bunk bed.

Andre shook his head as he pulled the last of the blinds off Mack.

"I couldn't get a hold of you!" Mack whisper-shouted. "What happened to your tablet?"

Andre blushed. "It broke—slipped out of my hands after a shower," he said. "I've been getting all my camp news bulletins from Benny."

Mack could've kicked himself. He looked from Andre to Miles to the boy looking down on him from the top bunk. *Benny.* He could've just emailed his old roommate for a Killington update, and saved everyone in the room a massive headache.

For a second, no one said anything, then Pat asked, "So, uh, what now? We have about forty-five seconds."

Mack stood to look Andre in the eye, rubbing his tail-bone. "We're here now, so we might as well ask," he said. "How are you?"

"Surprisingly good," Andre said. "The morning you left—"

"Why does everyone keep saying it like that?!" Mack interrupted.

"—everything changed. When kids found out why we were here and what we'd been going through, they

195

started treating me like anyone else. A bunch of them even joined Reo, Benny, and me for morning practice."

"Glad my leaving could help out," Mack said flatly.

"How are *you*?" Andre asked.

Miles gulped. "We sort of forced him into the middle of a bet with the Hortonia guys," he said.

"What kind of bet?" Andre asked.

"A ball-hockey game," Miles answered.

"What are the stakes?"

"Our cabin," Pat chimed in.

Andre whistled. "Good luck with that."

"Mack," Benny cut in, climbing down from his bed, "I want to apologize. The other day, I thought you were just trying to ditch us. I didn't know about everything else."

Mack waved him off. "*I'm* the one who's sorry. I should've said goodbye. No matter what else was going on."

"No, *I'm* sorry," Pat said.

Everyone in the room turned to look at him.

"For being so good-looking." Pat kissed his own shoulder but accidentally sucked in a few stray pine needles in the process. He began to cough lightly, then turned away, red-cheeked and angry at having ruined his own joke.

"That's our cue, I think," Mack said buoyantly.

He bumped fists with Reo and Benny, then turned to

Andre and raised his hand high. Andre slapped it, and the two engaged in their patented full-body shrug.

"See you soon," Mack said.

"See you soon," replied Andre.

CHAPTER
25

"WHAT'S GOTTEN INTO HIM?"

"Will someone please find out who's making terrible bird calls in front of our cabin?!" shouted one of Cassie's counselors in a gravelly voice.

It was 6:30 in the morning, and Cassie woke with a start. Terrible bird calls? This early?

"I'll do it," she said.

She slipped out from under her covers and walked to the front door. On the porch she found Mack, standing casually with his hands behind his back.

"Sounds like your counselor would get along with Laker," he said, smiling.

Mack stepped aside so Cassie could see Miles and Pat, who waved. All three boys looked tired and smelled like a campfire, but their eyes were energized.

"Let's go, Coach," Mack said.

Cassie rubbed her eyes. "Go where?" she asked.

"Practice," Mack said with a grin.

She raised her eyebrows. "But what about breakfast? I'm starving!"

"We raided the overnighter leftovers." Mack held out a clear plastic bag. "Brought you some hot dog buns."

"And marshmallows," Miles added.

"And marshmallows," Mack confirmed.

Cassie thought for a few seconds. "I'll give you this: you guys know how to make breakfast." She turned to address her cabin in a loud voice. "Cool if I go to the ball-hockey court to—"

"PLEASE!" shouted her counselor.

On the way to the court, the boys caught Cassie up on the events of the night. After leaving the Mendoza building, they had trudged back home along the road. Traffic had strangely picked up, which prompted several more trips into the ditch. By the time they got back to their tent, it was nearly 2:00 a.m. They were tired and dirty, and they fell asleep without even closing the flap.

But Mack had woken up again at 6:00 a.m. on the dot.

"We had stuff to do," he said nonchalantly, biting off a piece of hot dog bun.

"Yeah," Pat said. "Like sleep."

"You can sleep next week," said Cassie, now slightly nourished and ready to go. "We've got a job to do."

She looked at Mack, who was raising his hand.

"I'm not sure if you noticed this the other day," he said, "but I have no idea what I'm doing out there."

"That's my fault," she said. "I think my jump-into-the-deep-end strategy was a little ... uh, rushed."

This time, Cassie started Mack and Miles out easy, getting each boy to move back and forth across the court while controlling a ball with his stick. Miles took to it more quickly, but Mack stuck it out.

"What's gotten into him?" Cassie asked Miles during a break that Mack spent whipping wrist shots against the boards and trying to corral the rebounds.

"He's finishing what we started," Miles said, smiling.

After breakfast, Nicole, Makayla, Spike, and Mike showed up at the court—and Laker took a seat in the bleachers. The first drill of the morning focused on defensive positioning. As the forwards passed the ball around the perimeter, Cassie pointed to different spots on the ground.

"Cut off the shot, Mack!" she shouted.

Mack sprinted to the spots, sweat dripping off his face as he went.

"Now apply some pressure!" she shouted as he hedged toward the shooters and poked at the ball with his stick. "Don't just let them stand there."

Soon, Cassie noticed Mack making the correct reads

on his own—getting between the shooter and the net, careful not to crowd his defense partner or block Pat's view entirely. He even managed to get between players a few times and knock their passes away.

"Stop taking it so easy on him!" Cassie shouted to the forwards. "Make him work for it!"

Nicole, Miles, and Makayla picked up the intensity—making harder and quicker passes, testing his ability to stay in front of them—and so did Mack. He got beaten a few times by a pass skirting around him or a forward deking him out, but he'd learned to keep his head up until the ball went in the net—which it rarely did. Pat was nearly unbeatable, and Mack came to expect rebounds, which he would smack out of the danger zone in front of the net.

"Yeah!" Cassie encouraged. "That's it! Start the rush to the other end!"

Cassie watched Makayla chase a ball Mack had cleared and smiled. She was doing it. Her team was *learning*.

Makayla corralled the ball with her stick and turned back to the net, only to find Mack had followed her. He poked the ball between her legs and chased it across the center line toward the empty net at the other end.

"Go for it, Mack!" shouted Miles.

"Whose team are you on?!" Makayla fired back, only half playfully.

Mack stickhandled the ball across the blue line, separated his hands on his stick deliberately, and took a huge slap shot. He made great contact with the ball, which flew through the air … and passed three feet wide of the net.

Okay, Cassie thought, *so we still have some work to do.*

"Any day now!" someone shouted from the side of the court.

She looked over to see the Hortonia kids, led by Garth and Alexei, waiting impatiently. She checked Miles's watch and was amazed to see that her team had been on the court for nearly three hours. It was nearing lunch and long past time for them to surrender the playing surface to their competitors, who'd scheduled a solo practice of their own.

Cassie called her teammates together, told them that was enough for now, and followed them over the boards.

"All yours," she told Garth as she passed, giving him a sneer.

CHAPTER
26

"ARE YOU GETTING THIS?"

Exhausted, Mack flopped down next to Pat on the bleachers. After three hours on the court with only a marshmallow-hot-dog-bun sandwich in his stomach, his legs could barely hold him up anymore.

"Well, this was fun," Pat said dejectedly.

Mack furrowed his brow. The statement had sounded neither sarcastic nor sincere.

"What do you mean?" he asked. "What was fun? Or not fun. Or whatever."

"This," Pat said, raising his hand and gesturing all around without taking his eyes off the action. "This whole 'trying to win at ball hockey' thing."

"But …" Mack looked around him. He saw Cassie in animated conversation with Spike and Mike, and Nicole and Makayla comparing grips on their sticks. "But we're improving!" Then he had a thought. "We *are* improving, right?"

"It's not you," Pat said in a melancholy tone. "You're

doing great. It's …" He pointed at the court, where the Hortonia kids had dispensed with their warm-up and moved straight to scrimmaging.

Mack watched Garth score on a wraparound goal. Then he won a face-off, barreled through the defense, and with a simple flick of the wrists, sent a shot whistling past the goalie into the top corner of the net.

"The Hortonia team's good, but Forehead … he's great," Pat said.

Mack had to admit: even to his incredibly untrained eye, Garth was the best player out there. But after a moment, he stopped watching the court and started watching *his friend* watch the court. Gone was Pat's ever-present good humor—his way of always rooting out the joke or waiting to tell it. Pat didn't seem to find any of this funny. He seemed scared.

"No matter how much you guys improve between now and the big game, it's going to come down to me and him," he said.

Mack had encouraged Pat before, and he knew which buttons to push. "What about your silver medal?" he asked. "From the Swish City tournament?"

"I'm wearing it under my shirt. It's not helping," said Pat, hooking a thumb under the ribbon around his neck so Mack could see it. "I don't even know what Garth is going to do most times he has the ball, let alone how to keep him from scoring."

That could be fixed, Mack thought, *if we had a month to prepare.*

If they could only stop time, break down Garth's movements, watch them in slow motion, and—

Mack's eyes lit up. He stood and scanned the area until he found what he was looking for: Nelson and Wi-Fi standing along the boards. They were using their tablet to follow the action on the court, tracking the bouncing orange ball wherever it went.

Pat looked at Mack's delighted expression and furrowed his brow. "Glad someone is enjoying my funeral," he said dourly.

"Stay here," Mack said. "*This part* I might be able to do something about."

He climbed down the bleachers and approached Nelson and Wi-Fi from behind.

"Hey, are you getting this?" he asked.

The two boys jumped, nearly losing hold of the tablet.

"Obviously," Wi-Fi said, regaining his composure. "What do we look like, amateurs?"

Mack eyed the pair coolly. They were wearing wrinkled camp shirts and shorts and filming a ball-hockey practice with a tablet.

"Do you really want me to answer that?"

"Ouch," said Nelson.

"Hey, man, we're glad you're back and everything," Wi-Fi added, keeping the tablet's camera trained on the action, "but you're kind of killing our vibe."

"I'll make you a deal," Mack said. "Film the rest of this practice and send me the video file, and I won't bug you again."

Wi-Fi looked over his shoulder to make quick eye contact with Nelson. Then they both looked at Mack.

"Not a chance," said Wi-Fi.

"Deal," said Nelson.

The two boys shared another glance.

"Sorry. Still working on my eye-contact communication," Wi-Fi confessed. "Deal."

CHAPTER
27

"TODAY'S WINNER IS ..."

"Consider it done," Andre said into his brand-new tablet, which Killington tech support had delivered that afternoon. "Just send me the file, and I'll make it happen."

Andre ended the call and grabbed his dinner jacket from the closet. After the late-night visit from his old campmates, he had fallen back into a fitful sleep. At midday, he'd boarded a bus to Roundrock—the area's best basketball camp and the winner of last summer's Swish City tournament—for the first senior baseball matchup of the season.

Batting from the fifth spot in the order, he had gone three for four with two doubles and a home run in a 7–2 victory.

Now it was his night in the Ruth building, which made it easier to get ready for dinner. He donned the spotless black jacket in front of the full-length mirror with a look of distaste. There was nothing wrong with it, he thought—it just wasn't him.

Andre left the room, shutting the door behind him, and walked out of the building onto dorm row. The days of kids staring him down or giving him the cold shoulder were long gone. Now they gave him nods or high fives or looks of awe. House had made a point of putting him first in every drill they did since Mack got kicked out, and none of his campmates had made a single peep about it.

In fact, once the Killington kids had finally accepted him as one of their own, he had become nearly as big a celebrity as Deets himself.

"Nice game, Andre," peeped a junior camper staying in the Dietrich building.

"What do you know about it?" chided the boy's friend. "You weren't even there."

"I saw the box score," whined the boy.

Andre gave the boy a fist bump—"Thanks, man"— then joined a group of other senior campers on their way to the clubhouse.

Food began arriving as soon as Andre took a seat at his usual table. Having eaten lasagna ten times over the first few weeks of camp, he'd decided he needed a change. So in short order, he had a different dish placed in front of him: *Mexican* lasagna. His mouth watered when the scents of chili powder and homemade corn tortillas hit his nostrils.

But as was still the custom, he couldn't dig in until Deets did. He looked up at the boy in question—who, as it turned out, was looking at him.

"What?" Andre asked. "Am I slobbering?"

Deets smiled. "What's got you so giddy?"

"You mean, besides the Mexican lasagna?"

"Yeah."

"And going three for four?"

Deets gave him a look of appraisal. He had matched Andre's output with three hits of his own. "I rode the bus with you after the game," he said. "This is something else."

Andre could feel the entire room turning to look at him now. He wrestled with a decision: Blend in or be honest …

Blend in or be honest …

Be honest.

"I was talking to Mack," he said.

Andre heard more than a few gasps. Someone nearby sucked in breath through a closed throat. It was the first time Mack's name had been uttered in the clubhouse since he'd abruptly disappeared.

"My old campmates are playing Hortonia in ball hockey with their cabin on the line," Andre continued. "Game's in a few days."

"Bad move on their part," Deets said, grinning

maliciously as he picked up his knife and fork. "They're going to get creamed."

Andre grinned back. "I disagree."

All eyes locked on Deets as he hovered his silverware over the salmon steak in front of him. All hands reached for their own forks, knives, and spoons in anticipation. But then Deets leaned back in his chair, dropping his hands to either side of his plate with a clatter.

"Oh, come on!" whispered a small voice at the other end of the room.

Deets cast an angry sideways glance before resuming his line of questioning. "How *is* Mack at ball hockey?"

Not sure how or why, Andre suddenly felt locked in a high-stakes battle of wits. He and his rival were playing at something—and *for* something.

"Not great," he said.

Deets raised an eyebrow. "And the rest of the team?"

"They're okay, I think."

Deets laughed a laugh that no one joined in on. He drew in a breath, seemingly on the verge of saying something else, then abruptly jabbed a fork into his salmon with a motion that made the two kids closest to him jump.

CLINK!

He cut a chunk from the edge and jammed it into his mouth, cuing dinner for everyone else as well.

Guess someone doesn't like being disagreed with, Andre thought.

After dinner and dessert, Maxwell stepped to the front of the room.

"Just wanted to say a quick congratulations to the senior team for the resounding victory over Roundrock earlier today," he said. "And now for the game MVP presentation."

After each game of the summer, the camp director presented an award—a navy-blue T-shirt reading "I'm Going MVPro"—to the player whose performance he deemed most valuable.

"Today's winner is …"

As Maxwell paused for effect, Andre prepared himself. He knew the game MVP would be Deets. It was apparently *always* Deets.

"Terry Dietrich."

"DEEEEEEETS!" shouted the many kids in the room as they clapped and cheered. Andre joined in on the applause—Deets *had* had a great game—before Maxwell said something else.

"And Andre Jennings," the camp director shouted, holding up two of the coveted T-shirts. "Today we have co-MVPs."

The room fell into absolute silence.

For exactly one second.

Then it exploded in applause again.

"DRAAAAAAYYYYYYYY!" shouted the campers instinctively.

Andre blushed as he and Deets went up to collect their shirts. They received back pats and fist bumps from the camp director and the other coaches, and more from their fellow campers as they returned to their table.

Once outside, though, Andre felt Deets's large hand encircle his upper arm, stopping him in place as the other kids carried on down the path away from the clubhouse.

"What we were talking about before," Deets said as the area quieted. "The ball-hockey game between Average and Hortonia. Care to make that interesting?"

"It already is interesting," Andre said.

"What I mean is," Deets said, "wanna make a bet of our own?"

"Maybe." Andre cracked his knuckles absentmindedly. "I named the terms last summer. It's your turn."

Deets rocked back on his heels, his hands behind his back. "How about double or nothing?" he asked. "Hortonia wins, you do one more summer here. Camp Average wins, you can leave whenever you please."

Andre eyed him coolly. "Why do you even want me to spend another summer here? It's pretty clear you don't like me."

Deets smirked. "I brought you here to *mess with you*. Keep your enemies closer and all that. Not sure if you noticed, but I kinda told House I'd get him fired if he didn't submarine you and Mack."

"We noticed," Andre said flatly. "I also noticed he stopped answering your calls and yet he's still around."

"I was bluffing," Deets said. "He's too good a coach to get fired."

"Did you get the other campers to mess with us, too?"

"Nah. They were just following my lead." Then he added, "Until they weren't. Calling in a favor to get rid of Mack may have been a step too far."

Andre clenched his jaw, choking down his anger. "So what's left, then? Kind of sounds like we're done here."

"Oh no. Not even close." Deets rolled his eyes condescendingly. "I may have run out of ways to hurt you, but I'm still enjoying the motivation of having you around. No offense to anyone else here, but they're not in our league."

Andre shook his head. "We disagree about that, too," he said. "But it's a bet. Camp Average wins, I walk."

Deets snorted. "That'll never make sense to me," he said. "This place has better coaching, better facilities. You're better off here."

Again Andre shook his head. "You wouldn't get it."

The two shook hands.

"Easy money," Deets said. "There's no way that—"

"Sorry, man," Andre interrupted, taking off after his fellow campers. "Something I gotta do."

Running full speed, he caught up to the group in seconds. He found Reo and threw an arm around his shoulder.

"Congrats on the MVP," Reo said. "Just don't think about going back on your word to share *our* room."

"Funny you should mention that. How would you like to take my share of the nights in that room," Andre asked, "for the rest of the summer?"

Reo raised an eyebrow. "What's the catch?"

"I need a favor," he said. "For a mutual friend."

CHAPTER
28

"WE HAVE *NO* SHOT HERE!"

With glazed eyes, Mack pushed a pancake around his plate like he was stickhandling a ball. It was game day. He had spent the past few days in constant ball-hockey practice.

And it was clearly getting to him.

He'd taken instruction from Cassie, Pat, and whoever else was willing to work with him—even Laker had stayed awake long enough to assess his poke-checking progress. Collectively, they had decided to focus on his passing and defense.

"You don't have to learn how to score," Cassie had said. "You just have to learn how to get in the way."

When he and his friends didn't have the court, Mack ran wind sprints on the junior-camp field or smacked a ball against the side of the fieldhouse. At night, Miles drilled him on the rules and finer points of the game. He even read *For Those About to Hock*.

And yet, in the back of his mind, he felt certain he was

going to let his teammates down. He just didn't want to let them down *that much.*

Mack walked to the court in a fog and arrived to find a handful of early birds already there to claim seats in the bleachers.

As planned, he and his teammates were dressed in orange camp T-shirts, and their opponents wore plaid jerseys. Even Hortonia's coaches were sporting plaid.

With each team taking up one half of the court, the warm-up sped by. Then Simon, who was refereeing the contest as he had the kids-vs-counselors game, shouted for the teams to return to their benches before the opening face-off.

Mack heaved a large sigh and trotted over to the bench, where he found a nervous-looking Laker, who suddenly seemed very invested in being the team's coach. He was gnawing at his fingernails and bouncing his knee at the same time.

"Well, here goes nothing," Mack said, patting one of his teammates on the shoulder.

Except it wasn't one of his teammates.

It was Alexei.

Mack wasn't the only one who'd noticed the Hortonia player standing with the Camp Average kids.

"Wrong side, dude," Garth shouted from his side of

the court. Then he motioned like a bullfighter. "Come on! Let's go."

Alexei didn't move. "I'm good," he said.

Jaws dropped on the Camp Average bench.

"You're playing with *us*?!" Cassie said in a hushed tone.

"And you can speak English!" Pat shouted.

Alexei shot Pat a puzzled look. "What made you think I couldn't speak English?"

"You not speaking. At all. All summer."

As it became clear that Alexei really had switched sides, Garth took two steps forward, his cheeks burning.

"This is so uncool," he snapped.

"What? That I'm playing for Camp Average?" Alexei asked. "I sleep in a Camp Average cabin. I eat in the Camp Average mess hall." He pointed at Garth. "So do you, for that matter. You just haven't acted like it."

"Oh, come on, is this about—"

"We're number two," Alexei said softly, looking Garth in the eyes. "We're number two."

Mack knew the words—it was Camp Average's famous chant. He just couldn't believe where those words were coming from. But he joined in all the same.

"We're number two," Alexei said again, and the chant quickly spread to his new teammates and into the crowd. "We're number two! We're *number two*!"

In the bleachers, Nelson and Wi-Fi turned their tablet camera on themselves. "WE'RE NUMBER TWO! WE'RE NUMBER TWO!"

The chant lasted a full two minutes. Once it had finally died down, Garth—motionless during the entire spectacle—pointed at Cassie. "You're going down."

"Meh," Cassie said, shrugging. "Probably."

That somehow made Garth even angrier. He stormed to his team's bench as Cassie huddled up her own teammates in a giant circle.

"Okay," she said, "that was pretty cool." She punched Alexei in the shoulder across the huddle. "If you were trying to replace Pat as my favorite person at camp, mission accomplished."

Cassie looked sideways at Pat, who shrugged.

"Same here," he said, throwing Alexei a punch of his own.

"But the fact is they still have way more Hortonians than we do," Cassie continued.

"Wait, did Mack write this pep talk for you?" Pat asked. "This is classic Mack material right here."

Everyone looked at Mack, who put up his hands. "Innocent," he said. "This time."

He tightened a shoelace and tugged at his sweatpants, then looked up to find his teammates still staring at him. Waiting.

Mack's eyes bugged out. "Are you kidding me?! You want *me* to say something? I'm the worst player on the team."

"That's good." Pat grinned. "Go with that."

"Very funny!" Mack fumed. "So far this summer, I've spent two weeks at a snake pit of a camp, and then the snakes kicked me out. I learned to play ball hockey just a few days ago, and yet we're so thin, I'm a key cog in our attack. We have *no* shot here!"

He looked around at his teammates, who averted their eyes.

"Okay," Pat said, studying his shoes. "Maybe going with that was a bad idea."

Mack took a breath. He opened his mouth to apologize, but another voice broke the silence before he could.

"Let's go, Average!"

"Who—?" Nicole said.

She didn't have to wait long for her answer. From around the edge of the nearest cabin came Brian and Tamara, their old basketball coaches; Hassan, their old baseball coach; and Cheryl, their camp director. They'd all masking-taped the word "AVERAGE" to their orange staff T-shirts and smeared black face paint under their eyes.

Beyond them was a tall, athletic-looking kid in a turban.

"Slamar?!" Makayla exclaimed.

She was right. It was Samar Singh, the MVP of the Camp Roundrock basketball team, and he was followed by a few dozen of his campmates all dressed in red T-shirts.

Then Mack saw a wave of navy-blue shirts join the mix: Killington. He spotted Benny and Reo—plus one other very familiar face.

"Andre!" Miles shouted.

Andre burst out of the pack of kids like it was the final stretch of a race, and everyone in the stands reacted like he'd just won them a gold medal. As the bleachers continued to fill and cheers rained down, he sprinted around the ball-hockey court to the Camp Average bench.

"What are you doing here?" Mack asked as Andre hugged his old campmates. "What is *everybody* doing here?"

"Nelson and Wi-Fi's documentary," Andre answered.

Mack shook his head. "Sorry?"

"You guys didn't know?" Andre asked, smiling.

"We knew they were making a doc," Cassie said. "We just didn't know anyone else did."

"They posted a chunk of it to your YouTube channel a couple of days ago," Andre told Cassie. "My favorite part was when you rammed Mack's canoe and sent him flying."

Mack spotted Nelson and Wi-Fi in the bleachers, simultaneously high-fiving their loyal viewers and narrating the scene as they filmed it.

"At the end of the video, they included details on the game and a kind of open invite for any campers in the area. It took no convincing to get a couple of our coaches on board—I think they're subscribers."

"Of course they are," Cassie said, unsurprised.

"Even Deets wanted to come," Andre said, wrinkling his nose.

As if on cue, Deets walked into Mack's sight line, taking a seat on the bleachers behind them.

"Good luck, Mack!" he shouted. "I hear you'll need it."

Andre shot Deets a death stare, then motioned for Mack to follow him down the boards.

"I gotta tell you something," he said when they were out of earshot of both Deets and Mack's teammates.

"What?" Mack asked.

Andre's face cycled through a series of emotions. "I made a …" he started to say before trailing off. Then he shook his head. "You got this. That's all."

"Thanks, man."

Mack and Andre bumped fists, then Mack ran back to his teammates.

"Forget everything I just said," he announced.

"I wish I could," Pat said, grimacing.

"Just because this is impossible, that doesn't mean it's ..."

"Impossible?" Nicole asked.

Mack smiled. "Exactly."

The group dissolved in a series of hugs and high fives.

"Sure," Mack continued, "maybe we lose—"

"Stop while you're ahead, man!" Pat said as he slapped Alexei's back with both hands.

"Camp Aver—er, Avalon!" Simon shouted, breaking things up. "You ready?"

Mack looked around, suddenly aware of the crowd giggling at the aftermath of their pre-game speeches. He also saw the Hortonia players standing by their bench, staring at them with jaws clenched and nostrils flaring.

Then he turned to Cassie.

"Ready," she said.

CHAPTER
29

"I TAUGHT HIM THAT!"

Cassie stood with her knees bent and her upper body hovering over the face-off circle. Hovering over *her* was Garth. Despite being two years older, he was only a couple of inches taller. But he was easily forty pounds heavier.

Standing so close together as they waited for the ball to be dropped, the two looked more like helmeted wrestlers than hockey players, and the mental image lodged Miles's heart in his throat. That was partly out of worry for Cassie, and partly out of worry for himself. Cassie had asked him to start the game. And now he was standing to her left, ready to collect the ball if it bounced his way off the face-off. A Hortonia kid half a foot taller was positioned so close to him he could smell the bran flakes on the boy's breath.

Other than Mack, Makayla, and Alexei—who were all on the bench to start the game—the Camp Average players were lacking in size compared to the kids on the Hortonia team.

223

In other words, if this became a wrestling match, Miles didn't like their odds.

Further stacking the odds against them was the fact that Hortonia had nine forwards and six defenders—three full lines of players. Even with Alexei, Camp Average couldn't manage two. Cassie had updated their depth chart on the bench, but it still paled in actual depth compared to their opponents':

FIRST FORWARD LINE	NICOLE, CASSIE, ~~MAKAYLA~~ MILES
FORWARD SUBS	~~MILES~~ MAKAYLA, *ALEXEI!!!*
FIRST DEFENSE LINE	SPIKE, MIKE
DEFENSE SUB	MACK
GOALIE	PAT
GOALIE SUB	**STILL** DON'T GET INJURED, PAT!!!

Finally, Simon stepped past Miles into the fray. He had dressed up for the occasion in a black-and-white-striped ref shirt and had donned a helmet with no face cage.

"Okay, teams," he said in a soothing voice. "This is an intra-camp game, not a grudge match. And I expect everyone to act accordingly."

Cassie and Garth glared at each other.

"I'll blow my whistle for slashing, tripping, and so on," Simon continued. "Three minor penalties will get you kicked out. Are we clear?"

"Clear," Cassie said through her teeth.

"Sure," said Garth.

Simon produced the ball from the pocket of his black sweatpants, held it between Cassie and Garth for only a second, then threw it to the ground with a flick of his wrist.

The game was on. A portable digital scoreboard at the side of the court started counting down the first half.

Cassie and Garth jabbed at the ball with their sticks.

"GO, CASSIE!" Nelson shouted from the stands.

As if spurred on by her brother's support, Cassie pivoted to put herself between Garth and the ball. But Garth wasn't having it. He stepped beside her, knocking her sideways with his hip.

"Hey!" Miles shouted as Garth gained possession of the ball and passed it ahead to his right winger.

"It's legal, Miles!" Cassie yelled as she chased Garth into her team's zone. "I had the ball!"

Miles followed the play as the Hortonia players whipped passes around, looking for an opening, and Spike and Mike did their best to keep them at bay.

After the tenth pass, Hortonia's left winger fired a no-angle shot from twenty feet out that Pat easily snagged with his glove.

"Awesome job, defense!" Laker shouted from the bench, his voice somehow already hoarse. "Keep it up!"

Pat tossed the ball to Nicole behind the Camp Average net as Miles and Spike ran to the bench for a line change, bringing Alexei and Mack into the game.

"Here we go," Miles said, crossing his fingers.

But from the first moment, it was clear something had changed. Mack leapt over the boards without kicking so much as a single hair on Spike's legs, and he ran to the center of the court like he owned it. He stood firm, knees slightly bent, as he watched Cassie angle for a shot on goal.

Garth finally stole the ball and cleared it to his winger, who crossed the center line and, avoiding Mack, fired it all the way down the court so the Hortonia team could change lines.

On the bench, Miles felt a surge of pride. Had Mack not been in proper position, the winger wouldn't have dumped the ball—he would have charged in on a break-away. But Mack's very presence had persuaded him to give the ball away and let his team regroup.

As five fresh Hortonians leapt onto the court, Mack chased the ball behind the net, where it had come to a complete stop. Then he slowly and deliberately placed his stick on the ground behind the ball and used the blade to push it to Alexei, who had sprinted back to meet him. For all Mack's practice, his confidence with the ball on his stick hadn't improved much.

As Alexei carried the ball upcourt, the Camp Average kids made another change. Miles shifted over on the bench to make room for Mike and Nicole as Spike and Makayla jumped into the fray.

Pushing into the offensive zone, Alexei passed the ball to Cassie, who passed it right back. But Garth—blanketing his old teammate—snuck between them and stole the ball.

"That's what you get!" he yelled gleefully. With Spike caught out of position, he had just Mack to beat.

"Oh no, oh no, oh no!" Miles repeated at the coming confrontation as Mack retreated into his own zone.

Near the Camp Average blue line, Garth feinted to his right, forcing Mack to turn his shoulders. But when he deftly shifted the ball to his backhand and split left, Mack's feet got tied up underneath him, and he tumbled to the court.

"Ooooh!" said the crowd.

Mack shook off the mistake, getting up immediately, but Garth was gone. The only thing between him and a sure goal was Pat.

Garth barreled toward the left post as if he was planning to force the ball into the side of the net. But at the last possible second, he passed the ball sideways to himself and reached for it with his stick in one hand—trying to tap it into the right side of the net.

"Ooooooooooh!"

A few days earlier, the move would have worked. But today Pat was ready for it.

He stayed on his feet and tracked the ball across the crease, batting it away with his stick before Garth could even shoot it.

"Wha—?!" Garth grunted as his momentum carried him past the net.

The crowd erupted for Pat. In among the cheers, someone shouted, "I taught him that!"

Pat adjusted his mask as Spike cleared the ball, then pointed quickly up at the yelling kid. Basking in the glow of a job well done was Reo.

"What was that about?" Nicole asked Miles on the bench.

"Film study," he said with a grin.

For three straight nights, Pat had done nothing but video chat with Reo and watch the Hortonia practice footage that Nelson and Wi-Fi had recorded. The two boys had studied every frame, looking for patterns in footwork and body language that would tip off what move was coming. And now Pat knew more about Garth's repertoire than Garth did.

But unfortunately for Pat, Garth wasn't the only player on the team.

A few minutes later, while the star player was resting on the bench, Pat let a soft, low shot bounce awkwardly off his pads. A scrum formed around the goal mouth, and Pat lost sight of the ball.

"Where is it?!" the goalie shouted.

Finally, a Hortonia winger got his stick on the ball. It squirted out through a jumble of legs—and off the left post into the net.

PING!

"Goal!" shouted Simon.

"No!" shouted Pat.

A few minutes after that, Garth initiated a breakaway that led to a three-on-one against Mack. Pinpoint tic-tac-toe passing led to a wide-open shot that Garth put between Pat's legs as the goalie leapt from one side of the net to the other.

"Nooo!"

A minute after that, a Hortonia slap shot ripped into the top right corner of the Camp Average net.

"NOOOOO!"

"Don't worry about it, Pat!" shouted Cassie as she walked to the bench in the short break between goal and face-off. "Just get the next one!"

Miles watched as the team captain whispered something to Alexei, who nodded at her. Then Alexei nodded at his linemates, Miles and Makayla—a look on his face that said, "We got this."

Just a minute remained in the first half as Alexei secured the ball on the face-off. He passed wide to Miles, who darted under his check's arm to gain possession.

"Stop him!" Garth shouted from the bench.

The entire team seemed to zero in, but Miles got rid of the ball to Makayla before they could corner him. Makayla, in turn, passed to Alexei, who shook his check and unleashed a screaming wrist shot that beat the Hortonia goalie on his glove side.

"Goal!" shouted Simon.

"YES!" screamed the crowd as the first-half buzzer sounded.

Miles watched Alexei run along the bench, bumping fists with their teammates, who cheered the goal but couldn't match their fans' enthusiasm. The reason for the long faces was pretty clear in the digital red lights at the side of the court.

The score at halftime: 3–1, Hortonia.

CHAPTER
30

"EVERYBODY GOOD?"

"These guys are something else," Mack said on the bench as he tried to catch his breath and drink water at the same time. "They're incredible. They're—"

"They're no different from us," Miles said, cutting him off.

The two were sitting at the end of the bench away from their teammates.

"Come on, man!" Mack objected. "They're way better than—"

"I didn't say 'better.' I said 'different.'"

"I don't get it," Mack said.

Miles cleared his throat. He looked at the floor of the bench area. "We spend so much time talking about what we're not," he said quietly. "We're not the baseball camp. We're not the basketball camp. We're not the *ball-hockey camp*." He laced his fingers and set his hands in his lap. "I think sometimes we forget what we are."

"Which is what?" Nicole asked, inching closer with her teammates to listen in.

Miles looked her in the eye. "We're the pushback camp."

He scanned the kids around him, who were hanging on his every word. Even Laker sat in rapt attention.

"We're the figure-it-out camp," Miles continued. "We're the camp that doesn't care until things really matter—but then you'd better get out of our way."

Miles turned to Mack, who felt tears welling in his eyes. "I spent a lot of time this summer trying to be you," he said. "Trying to fix things all by myself. But it was an even bigger disaster than when *you're* you."

"Thanks," Mack said, casually brushing away a tear.

"I'm not you. And getting back to my point here—"

"Oh, there's a point?" Pat chided.

Miles looked down to the other end of the court, where the Hortonia players were warming up for the second half. "We aren't those guys—we *aren't* the ball-hockey camp. But it's like Cassie said in our cabin on the second day of camp." He turned to her. "Cassie?"

She furrowed her brow, trying to remember. Then a small smile crept over her face, and her eyes narrowed. "We're fighting for the soul of this place," she said.

The team fell silent, and Mack's eyes seemed to glow

as he looked at his teammates. Maybe they *couldn't* beat Camp Hortonia kids, he thought. But they could *be* Camp Average kids—at their very best—and live with the consequences.

◌◐

With Miles's words reverberating around the court, the team started the second half with wings on their sneakers. In minutes, Cassie split two defenders and beat the Hortonia goalie with a backhanded shot. Then Nicole scored on a breakaway to tie the game at three.

As she swooped back up the court pumping her fist, the crowd erupted in cheers. Nelson and Wi-Fi turned their tablet's camera on the stands around them, panning across the faces of dozens of screaming kids. Even the Killington campers seemed to be backing Camp Average.

"Nice shot, Nicole!" shouted Mack as he hopped over the boards for his shift.

But Hortonia wasn't done. After a quick, tense scrum to sort themselves out, they scored on a set passing play to pull back ahead 4–3.

That's how the score remained until the three-minute mark, when Hortonia again brought the pressure into the Camp Average zone. Garth pushed the ball up the court toward Mack, who retreated and waited for his opportunity.

As they crossed the blue line, Mack made his move, poking the ball away with his stick. But as he chased it, he felt something hit his right leg—hard. He stumbled forward but caught himself in time to avoid falling flat on his face.

"Hey!" Mack shouted.

TWEET!

"Garth!" yelled Simon, pulling his whistle from his lips.

"Forehead!" Garth corrected.

"That's a two-minute minor penalty for slashing!"

"Oh, come on!" Garth yelled. "My stick barely touched him. It was an accident!"

"Tell that to the welt Mack's going to have on his leg. You're just lucky I'm not giving you a major."

Garth slumped to his team's bench. Three minutes remained as Camp Average went on the power play with a one-player advantage.

"Now or never," Mack said, rubbing his leg.

Alexei won yet another face-off in the Hortonia zone and passed the ball to Miles. All three Camp Average forwards and two defenders formed a large semicircle around the Hortonia net. They passed the ball back and forth, looking for an opening as their short-handed opponents shifted to cut off any shooting lanes.

Finally, Miles passed from the left side of the court to Mack at the top of the semicircle. Seeing an opening, he reared back for a massive slap shot …

And missed the ball entirely.

The ball sped undeterred toward Makayla. Caught off guard, she swung wildly at it with both hands at the end of her stick. She connected, and the ball screamed through the Hortonia defensive zone into the top right corner of the net.

Simon knifed a hand out in front of him. "That's a goal! Tie game."

Makayla ran to the bench, where Nicole jumped over the boards to give her a hug. Then Nicole reared back and raised an eyebrow, a huge grin on her face.

"Okay, okay," Makayla admitted. "*That* looked like a golf shot."

Just a minute and a half remained. Mike and Alexei left the game, and Spike and Nicole entered it.

"Let's get one more!" shouted Cassie.

But getting another goal would prove difficult. As would simply touching the ball.

With Garth back in the game, the Hortonia forwards—who were fresher than the Camp Average kids, thanks to that third line—hammered shot after shot on net. Pat performed impressive acrobatics to get to the ball, but he couldn't seem to trap it in his glove.

Finally, with just seconds remaining on the clock, Pat stumbled going to his left. He blocked a wrist shot, but it bounced out in front of the suddenly empty net.

"Get the rebound!" Cassie yelled from the sidelines.

Mack was closest. He reached for it with his stick, but a Hortonia player got there first. He pulled it away from Mack and back to Garth, who lined up a slap shot—the same slap shot that had won him the right to stay in cabin 23 in the first place.

The ball rocketed off his stick toward the center of the net. It would go in for sure, unless …

"NOOOOOOOO!" Mack yelled.

He dove, his arms out in front of him like Superman.

SMACK!

The sound of ball on armpit echoed throughout the camp and the surrounding forests.

"Ow!" Mack shouted.

"Ooooooooh," the crowd groaned in sympathy.

As he landed on his hands and toes, the ball ricocheted off him toward the boards. The players chased after it, but it was too late.

BZZZZZ!

The clock showed zeros. The second half was over. And the score was still tied 4–4.

"We have overtime!" Simon yelled.

As their supporters screamed words of encouragement, the Camp Average kids ran to their bench one last time. All except Pat, that is, who waddled his way there.

Laker greeted them as they arrived. "Great work out there," he said. "You can do this."

"We *can't* do this," said Pat, breathing heavily. "I've got nothing left."

His teammates could tell he meant it.

"Well," Nicole said, "we got close. And maybe we can go double or nothing in a croquet match."

An image of a croquet pitch popped into Mack's mind as his teammates continued their nervous banter.

"What, and risk *our* cabin?" Makayla asked.

"Oh no." Nicole shook her head. "Who would be crazy enough to do that?" Then she looked at Cassie. "No offense."

"None taken. I mean, it wasn't *my* cabin."

Mack abruptly sucked in air. "Croquet," he said, staring off into the distance. Then he said it again, only more loudly. "Croquet!"

Pat waved his hand in front of Mack's glazed-over eyes. "Guys," he said between breaths, "I think we need to replace his batteries."

"Did you say …" Mike started.

"… croquet?" Spike finished.

Mack snapped out of it. "I did," he confirmed, breaking into a grin. "Miles, you got a piece of paper?"

෮෨

In two minutes, the players were back out on the court. Mack was joined by Cassie, Miles, Nicole, and Spike.

"Everybody good?" Mack asked, suddenly worried he was leading his teammates into disaster. He was hardly the biggest ball-hockey expert on the team.

"Good," said Cassie.

Near the face-off circle at center court, she grabbed Spike by the arm. "If I don't win this face-off, we're counting on you. Just don't let them shoot," she said, looking him straight in the eyes.

"I won't," said Spike without a hint of hesitation.

Cassie lined up opposite Garth. Simon held the ball out between them.

"This is sudden death," Simon said. "First goal wins. Good luck."

He dropped the ball, and Garth got to it first, pulling it back to his teammate. Cassie gave chase, but the ball was already pinging between players.

Mack backpedaled, keeping himself between the forwards and the net. But he didn't need to rush—the Hortonia players were advancing the ball slowly and deliberately, making sure to keep control until they could get a good shot on Camp Average's exhausted goalie.

Finally, they worked their way to within ten feet of the net. Mack raced out to try to steal the ball, but Garth deked him out, then passed it in front of the net, where two open teammates stood at the ready.

But they weren't actually open.

Spike emerged from behind them to cut off the pass and smack the ball to the edge of the playing surface. Mack watched as he raced after it, then whipped a pass up the boards to Nicole. She carried the ball to the Hortonia blue line and fired a perfect centering pass directly across the court, just in front of the goalie crease.

But there was no one there to receive it.

"Nice try, though!" mocked Garth.

The ball passed harmlessly by the crease, then landed on Miles's stick blade on the opposite boards. By now, both Hortonia defenders were giving chase, and the forwards were closing in as well.

Miles made a big show of looking worried, then heaved a pass all the way back down the court into his own zone, where Mack was waiting, again along the boards.

"Enough of this!" shouted a plaid-clad coach on the Hortonia bench. "Get the ball!"

The Hortonia players—Garth among them—swarmed toward Mack like bees.

Mack moved the ball back and forth in front of him with his stick, surveying the court. "Wait for it," he muttered to himself as they closed in. "Wait for it."

When the entire Hortonia team was practically on top of him, Mack let fly with a pinpoint pass—his finest of the summer.

To Pat.

For a split second, the crowd reacted like it was a mistake. A centering pass in front of his own net? Then the full situation became clear. Every Hortonia player was currently crowding Mack in one corner, leaving the middle of the court wide open.

Pat left his net, charging up the court in his goalie gear, the ball on his giant stick.

"GET HIM!" shrieked Garth.

Pat hit the ball ahead to Cassie, who cleanly gathered it and drove toward the Hortonia goalie. She wound up for a slap shot, fury in her eyes. Then she brought her stick down hard. The goalie tensed, ready to block the slap shot with his body.

But the slap shot didn't come.

Instead, Cassie lifted the ball off the ground, bounced it on her stick blade—once, twice—and batted it out of the air.

The goalie threw his gloved hand to his left, but the ball flew over it into the net.

Cassie dropped to her knees. "CROQUET!" she bellowed.

The Camp Average bench burst onto the court as the crowd erupted in cheers and stomps and applause and not a few confused looks.

Had she said "croquet"?

Mack grinned as he ran to join his teammates. His plan had worked. As the game had gone along, he'd noticed that the longer they managed to control the ball, the more frustrated the Hortonia players had grown. He knew that if they could play keep-away long enough, they might wind up with the entire team converging on a single player—which would leave the court wide open.

So they had gone up one side of the court, down the other, and back up the middle—just like a croquet player hitting the ball through the hoops in the correct order.

Mack reached Cassie and lifted her up in a bear hug. Then he felt someone try to pick him up. He looked around and found Miles.

"Great shot, Cassie!" he said. "It's just—"

"What?" Cassie said.

"I don't think they yell 'croquet' in croquet."

"Then what do they yell?" Pat asked, jumping in place as he threw off his goalie pads.

"They don't yell," Nicole said, joining the group along with Makayla, Alexei, Spike, and Mike.

"WELL, THEN, I GUESS WE CAN'T PLAY CROQUET!" Pat shrieked, throwing himself into the mix.

Onto the court rushed dozens of their campmates. Nelson and Wi-Fi even put down their tablet to join the revelers. And though their counselors—aside from Laker—hadn't been aware of the stakes, they all cheered along as if they understood the importance of the game.

Meanwhile, Mack's options for the rest of his summer flashed before his eyes in a series of images. Speedboats. Water skis. Canoes. Kayaks. Pool noodles.

He looked at Miles. Maybe a rocket launch. Maybe.

"Hey, Mack," Cassie said, pumping her fist. "See you at practice tomorrow?"

Mack smiled. "Not a chance," he said.

EPILOGUE

"A DEAL IS A DEAL"

After the on-court celebration died down, Mack walked the length of the Hortonia handshake line until he got to the final person in it: Garth.

Instead of holding out a fist to bump, the Hortonia captain held up both hands as the Camp Average players massed around him.

"A deal is a deal." He looked at Pat. "I was wrong about you the whole time, and I'm sorry about all the poison ivy." He turned to Cassie and Alexei. "And about … the other stuff."

"You should be," Cassie said.

"It's cool," added Pat.

Alexei stared blankly.

"So best friends?" Garth asked Pat, holding out his hand.

"Best friends," Pat agreed, shaking it.

"What?!" Miles grabbed his head in both hands. "You mean, after *all* that, you're just going to *become* best friends?"

Garth shrugged. "That was part of the deal. And you know what they say: Forehead's word is as strong as his slap shot."

"Nobody says that!" Miles yelled. "And nobody calls you that!"

"Hey," Pat said indignantly, putting a protective arm around Garth, "that's my best friend you're talking about. If he says his name is Forehead, his name is Forehead."

"Why do you even want to be called that, anyway?" Cassie asked.

"It sounds like Fortin," said Garth. "And it distracts from my nose."

"Doesn't really seem like it's catching on."

Garth shrugged again. "Wayne Gretzky says you miss one hundred percent of the shots you don't take."

"Wayne Gretzky never said that!" Cassie shouted. "Right, Miles?"

"Actually, I think he did say that one," Miles confirmed.

Slamar and the Roundrock campers came through for a round of high fives, and Slamar asked Nelson and Wi-Fi when the full documentary would be ready.

"The final night of camp," Wi-Fi told him proudly, holding the tablet in Slamar's face for a close-up. "Everybody's invited. Red-carpet debut."

"Without the red carpet," Nelson said.

Then Benny and Reo cut in to wrap Mack in a bear hug.

"Reo!" Mack wheezed. "I didn't take you for a hugger."

"We're not competing anymore," he said, loosening his grip. "Big difference."

"Hey," Benny said as they got ready to leave, "take care. And take care of Andre."

"We'll take care of his dorm room," Reo followed up.

Mack squinted. "What?"

Just then, he felt a hand on his shoulder. He turned to find Andre and Deets.

"Well, I'm happy to see one of you," Mack said, glowering.

"Hey now," Deets said, "that's not a nice thing to say to our friend Andre here. Especially considering he chose your camp over mine."

Mack searched Andre's face, which was betraying nothing. He looked at Benny and Reo, who also weren't offering any answers.

"Again," he said, "what?"

Andre broke into a smile. "I went double or nothing with Deets."

Mack furrowed his brow. "On what?"

"On you."

Mack blinked. "You bet an entire summer of your own freedom on us beating *Hortonia* … at *ball hockey*?"

"Yes."

"ARE YOU CRAZY?!"

"Maybe." Andre grinned. "But you told me Cassie, Pat, Spike, and Mike were good. And it's common knowledge that Nicole and Makayla can figure out any sport if you give them a minute."

"That's true," Nicole said as she and the rest of the team drew closer to listen in.

"But I didn't know that Alexei would wind up playing for you," Andre said. "And if he hadn't, well ..."

"You would've been destroyed," Deets interjected.

"That's not entirely fair," Mack said. "Pat killed in net, and Cassie coached us up."

"And if Nicole hadn't convinced Makayla to try croquet," Cassie added, "we never would have had that final play."

"Finally some credit!" Nicole shouted, placing a hand on Makayla's shoulder.

"This is what I'm saying," Andre continued. "When something matters, you guys find a way. And you did. So who's crazy now?"

"YOU ARE!" Mack shouted, grabbing his hair and spinning in place.

"Guess this means we're no longer campmates," Deets told Andre. Then, in a sarcastic voice, he added, "Bummer."

"No way, man!" Andre replied. "You don't get to sound like this was your plan. You wanted me to stay at Killington. You lost."

Deets burst out laughing. "How do you figure?"

"You lost the bet!" Andre looked around at his friends, who were equally confused. "You *lost* the *bet.*"

Deets waved a hand in the air. "Maybe, but I was gonna win no matter what," he said. "Now I get my camp back all to myself. I was tired of sharing top-dog status with you anyway. So I didn't lose anything."

"That's such a—" Mack started to say before Deets cut him off.

"See you around, *Mack.*"

Deets turned his back on the group and walked off, joining up with some Killington kids.

"What a sore loser," Pat whispered as Mack fumed.

Garth grunted his agreement. "Yeah, that dude really is number two." He looked at Pat. "Or is that not how that saying works?"

A few minutes later, Andre boarded the Killington bus, promising to return as soon as he could talk to his parents and make the switch. And if he got in a few extra sessions in the batting cage while he waited, he wasn't going to complain.

When they'd all finished waving goodbye, Miles

sidled up to Mack. "Speaking of sleeping arrangements," he said, "now that Andre's coming back, we don't have enough beds for everybody. It'd be wrong for Alexei to lose his after he helped us out."

"Didn't you guys hear?" broke in Laker, lugging a bag of hockey equipment around the side of the court. "Camp Hortonia is open for business. The renovations are done. Kids will start moving over there day after tomorrow, latest."

Nobody said a word as Laker trudged away.

"Well," Garth said finally, "now I don't want to leave."

Cassie smiled. "Nobody ever does," she said.

∞

The next morning, Mack left the mess hall for the water-front, a bright, multicolored beach towel around his neck. He had almost cleared the camp office when he heard a voice call his name.

"Hey, Mack!"

Mack's shoulders slumped. *So close*, he thought. He turned to find Laker, a knowing smile on his face.

"Got a second?" the counselor asked. "Cheryl wants to talk to you."

Mack did a double take. The camp director wanted to

248

talk to *him*? In his vast experience at Camp Average, that had never been a good thing. He searched his mind for recent offenses. Did she know about the ball-hockey bet? The secret mission to Killington? Or both?

"She wants to ask you something," Laker said.

"Oh, yeah?" Mack asked nervously. "What?"

"Have you ever considered becoming a junior counselor?"

PRAISE FOR *CAMP AVERAGE*

"Hilarious, irreverent, and timely, highly recommended for sports fans, summer-camp alums, and preteen-year survivors."
—*Kirkus Reviews*, STARRED REVIEW

"A great book about friendship and standing up for what you believe."
—*Pennsylvania School Librarians Association*
Teaching and Learning Literature Review

"A wild and wacky novel...that will delight young readers who want to relive their own camp experiences or summer camp wannabes."
—*The Globe and Mail*

"Young readers who are yearly campers, huge sports fans, or just looking for a solid story full of humour... will find something to love in *Camp Average*."
—*Canadian Review of Materials*

PRAISE FOR *CAMP AVERAGE: DOUBLE FOUL*

"A funny, satisfying exploration of the thematically rich territory between winning and losing."
—*Kirkus Reviews*

"A few surprising plot twists in this humorous, character-driven summer read show cooperation is always best."
—*Booklist*